LEFT

TO

LAPSE

(An Adele Sharp Mystery—Book Seven)

BLAKE PIERCE

Blake Pierce

Blake Pierce is the USA Today bestselling author of the RILEY PAGE mystery series, which includes seventeen books. Blake Pierce is also the author of the MACKENZIE WHITE mystery series, comprising fourteen books; of the AVERY BLACK mystery series, comprising six books; of the KERI LOCKE mystery series, comprising five books; of the MAKING OF RILEY PAIGE mystery series, comprising six books; of the KATE WISE mystery series, comprising seven books; of the CHLOE FINE psychological suspense mystery, comprising six books; of the JESSE HUNT psychological suspense thriller series, comprising fifteen books (and counting); of the AU PAIR psychological suspense thriller series, comprising three books; of the ZOE PRIME mystery series, comprising six books; of the ADELE SHARP mystery series, comprising ten books (and counting); of the EUROPEAN VOYAGE cozy mystery series, comprising six books (and counting); of the new LAURA FROST FBI suspense thriller, comprising three books (and counting); of the new ELLA DARK FBI suspense thriller, comprising six books (and counting); of the A YEAR IN EUROPE cozy mystery series, comprising three books (and counting); of the AVA GOLD mystery series, comprising three books (and counting); and of the RACHEL GIFT mystery series, comprising three books (and counting).

An avid reader and lifelong fan of the mystery and thriller genres, Blake loves to hear from you, so please feel free to visit www.blakepierceauthor.com to learn more and stay in touch.

BOOKS BY BLAKE PIERCE

RACHEL GIFT MYSTERY SERIES
HER LAST WISH (Book #1)
HER LAST CHANCE (Book #2)
HER LAST HOPE (Book #3)

AVA GOLD MYSTERY SERIES
CITY OF PREY (Book #1)
CITY OF FEAR (Book #2)
CITY OF BONES (Book #3)

A YEAR IN EUROPE
A MURDER IN PARIS (Book #1)
DEATH IN FLORENCE (Book #2)
VENGEANCE IN VIENNA (Book #3)

ELLA DARK FBI SUSPENSE THRILLER
GIRL, ALONE (Book #1)
GIRL, TAKEN (Book #2)
GIRL, HUNTED (Book #3)
GIRL, SILENCED (Book #4)
GIRL, VANISHED (Book 5)
GIRL ERASED (Book #6)

LAURA FROST FBI SUSPENSE THRILLER
ALREADY GONE (Book #1)
ALREADY SEEN (Book #2)
ALREADY TRAPPED (Book #3)

EUROPEAN VOYAGE COZY MYSTERY SERIES
MURDER (AND BAKLAVA) (Book #1)
DEATH (AND APPLE STRUDEL) (Book #2)
CRIME (AND LAGER) (Book #3)
MISFORTUNE (AND GOUDA) (Book #4)
CALAMITY (AND A DANISH) (Book #5)
MAYHEM (AND HERRING) (Book #6)

CHAPTER ONE

Lea Dubot reclined in the padded chesterfield, her head resting against the embroidered seams of swirling blue and white. Above her, a miniature chandelier dangled in the first-class compartment of the Normandie Express. She inhaled the soft odor of bourbon whose glass rested in the cup holder built into the tea table's frame at her elbow. Every so often, her gaze flitted from the glass baubles of the chandeliers hung throughout the lounging compartment and darted toward the dining car of the train, visible just through the glass partition at the end of the long compartment.

The train itself moved with a surprising quiet—top of the line soundproofing and muffled gear mechanics, according to the mechanical engineering student who was in the room next to Lea's. Normandie Express boasted a perfect blend of traditional comfort and modern amenities. On the inside of the car, it felt like something out of an old-fashioned movie, with a historic flair from the maps in the dining hall framed on the walls, to the tasseled throw pillows of pure cotton in the lounging area.

Across from Lea, an obviously wealthy lady was sipping from a steaming mug of some sort, muttering about the weather and causing the pearls encircling her neck to clack and shift as she fluffed her fur collar.

"Bonjour," Lea said, nodding and smiling. The woman had to be three times her age, but it didn't hurt to make conversation.

The rich older lady didn't reply. Instead, she turned slowly, her features moving like molasses finally settling in a pan. She inched a nearly nonexistent eyebrow up over a well-wrinkled eye, and then turned once again to peer out the window displaying French countryside to the north—mostly soft hills, green flatland, and a coastal vision of the English channel.

"It's a new train, you know," Lea said, quoting the engineering student again if only to make an impression. "It just *looks* old."

The woman sighed as if she couldn't quite be bothered to spare words, but managed to eke out, "Quite," in a creaking voice like an old

1

chestnut cabinet. Then she turned away again and Lea was left sitting in silence.

Lea sighed, but tried not to take it too personally. She had known it would take a day or two to make friends on the cross-country trip along Northern France into West Germany, then through Poland and Romania. Perhaps the engineering student was still back in the sleeping compartment.

She got to her feet, again surprised at how steady her stance was beneath her. She'd been on trains before, but never one this smooth. The floor itself was even carpeted with a Turkish rug.

She sent a forced little smile toward the standoffish older woman, then began to move toward the dining car, which would lead to the sleeping compartment. She pushed a hand against the door, but before she could press through, it swung inward, toward her, nearly knocking her from her feet.

"Sorry," came the flustered, muttered voice of a man in a black raincoat. He dipped his head apologetically, and she couldn't quite meet his eyes as he hurried past her.

She caught her balance against an ornamental trim circling the windows, and then, adjusting her sweater and shooting a reproachful glance back toward the woman who'd ignored her and the man who'd nearly bowled her over, she marched, chin high, through the compartment into the dining hall.

The ornate, hand-carved oak furniture alone would have been spectacle enough, but what really did it was the row after row of immaculate china—now set in a locked glass cabinet pressed to the far wall, but brought out for every mealtime.

Lea smiled as she moved along, nodding to a young Swedish couple from business class who were sitting in the dining car with one of their college-age friends.

As she maneuvered through the dining car, though, Lea froze, barely resisting the urge to curse. Her hand darted toward her elbow on instinct, feeling for the strap of her small clutch purse. Nothing. She glanced down and confirmed.

"Merde," she muttered, quiet enough so the others couldn't hear. She did an about-face, then marched back toward the compartment she'd just left to retrieve her forgotten belongings.

As she moved along, pushing back through the glass partition into the lounging area, she frowned. The old woman was still sitting in her pearls and silks on the chesterfield facing the largest window. But the man in the black raincoat had somehow vanished. She peered past the woman toward one of the windows, now open and letting a breeze through, accompanied by the chugging sound of the train.

Leah shook her head and moved to where she spotted her small brown purse resting against the arm of one of the recliners. She winced apologetically at the older woman, as if expecting her to sigh in frustration at the return of a nuisance.

But as Lea neared, the woman in question looked anything but annoyed.

The older woman's eyes were bugged; in one hand she gripped the coffee mug she'd been sipping. A second later, the mug fell, smashing on the ground and sending steaming liquid and fragments of porcelain every which way.

Leah blinked, her heart jarred, and she stammered, "Are you okay?"

And then, as if jolted by electricity, the older woman catapulted forward, lunging, as if spasming from the seat. She didn't make it far as her frail legs didn't have the strength, but one hand reached out, grasping desperately toward Leah. The older woman's fingers scrambled against Leah's arm, desperately trying to grip her, and Leah let out a soft scream.

The woman's mouth was half open, her eyes gaping like those of a fish.

"Oh," the older woman said. And then her hand, which had been pressing against Leah's, fell and pushed to her chest. "Oh," she repeated. And then she keeled over, collapsing to the ground, foaming from the mouth, and after shaking another couple of times, the older woman fell still, her circlet of pearls stained by strands of vomit.

Leah stared for a moment longer, and then, as if suddenly plunged into icy water, the reality of the situation struck her. She raised her voice, and at the top of her lungs, screamed in the old-fashioned train car, her clutch purse momentarily forgotten where it sat against the armrest.

CHAPTER TWO

"So what did you want to tell me?" said the Sergeant, raising a thick eyebrow and running a finger through his walrus mustache. Adele's father was wearing his trademark white T-shirt instead of a proper sweater. At least this time they weren't in the Alps, testing his ability to stave off the nip of cold on willpower alone.

Now, though, a familiar frown had crossed the Sergeant's countenance.

Adele wasn't sure if her father was more frustrated with returning to France, or because he'd traveled overnight at her insistent request. Now, in Adele's apartment, standing next to the large floor-to-ceiling window that led onto the small terrace and overlooked the city of Paris, Adele wasn't sure where to start.

Her own mind whirred, spinning in frustration at how she might broach the news. He wouldn't take it well. One way or another, she knew her father, and he wasn't going to like what she had to say. But what else was there to do except tell him?

"We came across Mom's killer," Adele murmured, slowly.

Her father's single carry-on item of luggage rested by his feet. He hadn't even had time to take a shower since arriving from the airport as he'd only been in her apartment for about ten minutes. But that was the way of things in the Sharp household. Straight to the point. Without much room for undertakings of affection or connection.

For a moment, Adele's mind wandered to her old mentor, Robert Henry. He'd been sick—very sick—but recently had shown some signs of mild improvement. The thought alone weighed heavy on her heart, but she shook her head, focusing for the moment and trying to gauge her father's response to her words.

His face remained blank. "What do you mean?" he probed.

"I mean what I said," she replied. "Agent John Renee—do you remember him? He was working the case while I was…" Adele hesitated and trailed off.

"Taking a break," her father said.

Adele knew the danger of allowing her father to fill in her

4

sentences. There had been a time, not long ago, when given the opportunity, he might have said something like, "running away from your problems." Or, "having a mental breakdown."

Her father hadn't been one to mince words. But they were beginning to see eye to eye more and more. What they saw neither much agreed with, but at the very least, they were beginning to understand how to relate. Or so she hoped.

Then again, the Sergeant had withheld evidence in her mother's case, and Adele was still having a hard time looking at him the same way she had before. Still, he had loved Elise once upon a time and despite how things had ended between them, Adele knew he'd taken her murder very poorly. He deserved to know.

"He saw the killer? And did he *catch* the killer?" Still no expression.

"He tried, but failed to snag the bastard."

"Adele," her father said, sharply. "Language."

She rolled her eyes. Some things never changed. "Fine. He failed to catch the *killer.* John had to save a victim." She said this part with pursed lips, her voice tight. She had already been over it with Renee, and didn't feel like getting into it with her father as well.

For his part, the Sergeant's calm façade was cracking a bit. His eyebrows bunched lower, but even more so, a quiet storm brewed in his gaze. They were darker than she remembered, and his pupils almost seemed dilated. He was breathing in shallow puffs, and she noticed one of his hands had clutched the edge of his shirt, pulling on the white fabric.

"He saw his face, briefly, and got a look at his physique. He's going to try to work with a composite artist," Adele said, speaking as matter-of-factly as she could muster. Inwardly, her own stomach twisted and turned. She remembered her conversation with Renee, the flash of anger. Then the subsequent regret at how poorly she'd treated him. Clouding it all, though, had been the cold certainty: the killer was still out there, laughing in the dark. She cleared her throat, closing her eyes to steady herself for a moment, then continued, "It doesn't look promising. And either way, I think the killer was spooked. Whatever he was up to, ducking out of cover, he's going to stay in hiding for a lot longer this time."

The Sergeant crossed his arms and growled, "Why did he let him get away?"

5

"Like I said, he had to choose between saving a victim and catching the killer."

A sudden jolt of rage displayed across the Sergeant's face, twisting his expression and causing a growling, barking sound to explode from his lips as he snarled, "Catching the killer *would* save lives."

Adele shrugged sympathetically. "I know."

Her father seemed to lose some steam now, and he collapsed in the couch facing the window, leaning back, his walrus mustache facing the ceiling fan.

"What do you mean you think he's gone?"

"I mean, John saw him. Not well, and in the dark, but the bast—er, *killer* would be stupid to try anything else."

"If you caught him once, you can do it again, can't you?"

Adele winced and shrugged. "I don't know if it's going to be that easy. Look how long we've been searching so far, and only now did we stumble upon anything at all."

Her father exhaled through his nose. "Well, he will have to remember then, won't he. Whatever he saw. Your friend—this John. He has to remember."

"It was dark. He only caught a glimpse. I don't know what's going to come of it."

The Sergeant shook his head, frowning. "Anything else I should know?"

Adele sighed. "Nothing I can think of. Things got a little bit quiet after that. It was only a week or so ago. I had to see if I could follow up on any leads, but nothing came of it." Adele paused, then said, "One of the cafeteria workers on the first floor at DGSI vanished about a week and a half ago. But her family says it's not uncommon for her to go off traveling with some out of town boyfriend for the fun of it. We're looking into it, but other than that, things have been calm."

"A cafeteria worker vanished? Not retaliation for seeing his face, is it?"

"No body," Adele said, wincing. "Like I said, they're keeping an eye out."

"Dammit," said the Sergeant. He sat in silence for a moment, his head still reclined, still pressed into the couch.

Through the window, Adele watched as traffic moved through the streets of Paris. She breathed slowly through her nose, steadying her nerves by focusing on the exhalation.

She wasn't sure what else to do. "I have a spare pillow and some blankets in the cupboard in the hall. You're welcome to it. Stay as long as you like," she said, not because she really meant it—but because she knew her father, like her, would want to spend as little time as possible in the same cramped space as they could manage.

It wasn't that she didn't love her father. It was that she didn't know how to express it. And either he suffered the same difficulty, or had never learned how to kindle affection in the first place.

Either way, now that she'd said it, she wasn't sure what to add. "I have some cereal in the cupboards," she continued, hesitantly. "And I also—"

Before she could finish, her phone began to ring, chirping from her pocket with quick, punctuated sounds like a twittering bird.

"Sorry," she said with a wince. Quickly, she answered, turning a shoulder to her father's seated form. "Yeah?"

The voice on the other end replied, "Adele..." It was John, and Adele went suddenly stiff. She hadn't left things with her old partner in a particularly healthy place.

"Yeah?" she said; the word had worked the first time, and she saw no reason to change it.

"Foucault wants us both in. A new case."

Adele swallowed, trying to compose herself. For a moment, she had hoped John was calling for personal reasons.

"All right," she said, "when?"

"Right now. Urgent."

"I'm with—with my dad."

"Germany?"

"No, he's here. He just got in."

"You want me to tell the Executive—?"

"No, no," she said, quickly. "I'm on my way."

She hung up and glanced at her father, flinching. If he'd been listening at all, he didn't show it. His head was still tilted, his eyes fixed on the ceiling, his arms splayed out across the top of the couch, his chest rising and falling slowly beneath the thin fabric of his white T-shirt.

"Work," she said, hesitantly.

At first, he didn't seem to be aware he was being addressed.

"Dad, I've gotta go in to work."

He looked over now, his eyes cloudy, some of the darkness she'd seen before having faded, as if to be replaced by a sudden stupor. He murmured something softly, then shook his head.

"I'll try to get back as soon as possible," she said, wincing. "Feel free to order food or raid the fridge. Whatever you want."

Her father looked at her for a moment, his eyes sad in a way she wasn't accustomed to. The normally rigid and rough man before her looked raw, exposed, as if a veneer had suddenly been stripped away. She saw a naked look of grief in his eyes, for a moment, and she wasn't sure she wanted to stay near it.

At last though, he shook his head and sighed. "You know… you got closer than I ever could," he said, and for a faint moment a smile even crossed his normally dour expression. "As Yogi Berra said, 'It ain't over till it's over.'"

Adele blinked. She wasn't sure what a cartoon bear had to do with it… Was she remembering that name right? No matter. But despite her father's words, his eyes still held another trait… something deeper, darker, lurking behind his gaze. "Go," he said. "I'll be fine. I'll see you tonight."

"You sure?"

"I'm sure. Duty calls."

She shook her head hesitantly, then muttered another apology, hating that she was leaving her father only a half hour after he'd arrived. She sighed, waited to see if he'd say anything else, and when no words were forthcoming, she quickly marched to where she'd left her keys and wallet, snagged them, gave one last, "See you in a bit," and then, grateful for the excuse, she hurried out the apartment door, shutting and locking it behind her. A new case would provide a distraction. And right now that's exactly what she needed.

CHAPTER THREE

Adele took the elevator from the bottom floor of the DGSI headquarters in that strange, pink building outside the old café. The headquarters was a relatively new structure as was the agency itself.

As the elevator doors dinged, passengers got on and off, carrying with them—from the adjoining corridors—the smell of fresh coats of paint, where workers were still completing the building over a contract that seemed like it might take twenty years thanks to a combination of slow workers and ridiculous security protocols hampering the painters' workdays and personnel.

Not every part of the DGSI, though, was so guarded. Adele thought briefly of the basement. John Renee liked to keep his own speakeasy down there, a hidden bachelor pad. She'd been invited into the sacred space more than once, but not recently. Recently, things between them had been less than ideal.

She took the elevator to the second floor first, adjusting the sleeves of her suit and smoothing a lock of blonde hair behind an ear. Adele bid a quick farewell to the two other passengers still waiting in the elevator, and then stepped out onto the carpeted hallway. She moved rapidly toward Robert Henry's spacious office which overlooked a portion of the parking lot and a view of the distant city.

Renee had said the meeting with Foucault was urgent, but Adele still couldn't shake thoughts of her old mentor. What could it hurt just to check in quickly? Just to see his smiling face, to see how he was doing?

As she neared Robert's door, though, she noted it was closed. Adele frowned, glancing up and down the hall. She tapped delicately on the door. No answer.

She knocked a bit louder, then tried the handle. Locked.

"Robert?" she called.

A head poked out from the doorway across the hall, and a woman with short hair frowned. "He's sick," she said. "Didn't come in today. Please keep it down."

Adele winced in apology and then turned, moving dejectedly back

9

to the elevator. Robert had been coming in to work over the last week as much as possible. If he hadn't come in today, his health must have declined again.

She gave a shuddering little breath that rattled her throat before boarding the elevator again. She made a mental note to visit Robert as soon as possible.

Adele took the elevator one floor up, to the third level, and the doors dinged open, revealing another carpeted hall. Adele walked briskly toward a bench which faced an opaque door.

For a moment, she stopped. Normally, John Renee would wait for her outside the Executive's door. It had been a ritual of sorts. They would often enter the room together, facing the wrath of the Executive with backup.

But now she could hear voices from inside, and the opaque glass door was half ajar, suggesting John had already entered ahead of her.

Adele stepped away from the bench in the carpeted hall and pushed her fingers against the opaque glass. She hesitated, listening through the glass at the slow growl of Agent Renee's voice. For a moment, she felt a flash of recollection, how things had been left the last they'd spoken. How poorly she'd treated him and yet how angry she'd felt. Now, some of the anger had numbed, but the sheer pain, the grief of the situation, ten years in the making, wouldn't allow her to settle. Would John be angry to see her? Would he ignore her? How could she patch things up? Did she even want to?

She pushed against the glass at last and moved into the Executive's office. As she entered, she was struck by how it smelled.

Normally, Foucault's office would exude the aroma of an ashtray inside a dumpster full of cigarettes. He often opened the window when he smoked, but it didn't help things much.

Now, though, she could barely detect the scent of ash. Perhaps a faint bit had leached into the carpet and walls from years of abuse. But mostly, the odor she detected now was a surprisingly pleasant one, seemingly emanating from flickering red candles in rose cup glass containers placed around the desk.

Rather than smoking, as often was the case, Executive Foucault instead seemed to be chewing on something. Adele glanced at the desk and noted a pile of nicotine gum packs, with a thick, balled up circlet of wrappers forming somewhere near his open computer.

Agent Renee was in the room as well, sitting across from the

10

Executive's desk, shaking his head and muttering. As Adele entered, John fell quiet, as if sensing her, and turned, glancing in her direction. The tall, handsome agent had dark, slicked back hair and a strong nose. A twisting set of burn marks moved up like creeping ivy from his chest to the underside of his neck, then to his chin.

She felt a flutter of happiness at the sight of her old partner. She cleared her throat and dipped her head in a quick greeting. "Hello," she said. She'd intended for the word to come out more warmly than it had. John's expression didn't change, but he seemed to note the accidental coolness of her tone. "Good morning, Agent Sharp," he said, brusquely.

"Take a seat, Sharp," Foucault called from behind his desk. He popped another stick of nicotine gum in his mouth and gestured impatiently toward one of the chairs near where John sat.

"I'll make this quick," Foucault continued. The Executive of the DGSI had a hawklike nose and a dark brow. He was shorter than John and his voice came stained with the cigarette smoke normally found hovering throughout the poorly ventilated room.

Now, though, while the smoke was gone, replaced by flickering cherry candles, the strain in Foucault's voice only seemed to have increased. He also seemed to be perpetually glowering and reached up, rubbing at his temples.

"Is… is everything all right, sir?" Adele said.

"Fine," he snapped back. He followed her gaze, glancing to the stacks of gum packs and the candles. He sighed and waved airily. "Sorry. Just trying to kick a habit. New leaf and all. But we're not here to talk about me."

Adele settled in the seat next to John, all too aware he wasn't paying much attention to her. Was he intentionally neglecting her? Had they left things that rough after all?

She shot a look toward where the long frame of the tall agent reclined in his seat. He looked as bored as ever to have been dragged into a meeting. Normally, though, the boredom was a bit of a joke between them. She would often tease him about being unprofessional, and he'd respond by calling her American Princess or something equally condescending.

It was a playful banter that had seen Adele through some of the tougher days on the job. Now, though, he'd referred to her as Agent Sharp on entry, and his boredom seemed self-contained, shared only with himself.

11

Foucault's irritation did little to stem the tide of frustration rising in Adele's own chest, so she bit her tongue and waited.

"Two bodies, two countries," Foucault said, curtly, speaking around a wad of gum the size of a walnut. "Both of them having died of what appears to be a heart attack on two different trains."

"Trains?" said John.

"Trains."

"What type of trains?" Adele asked.

"The ones that go choo-choo and sit on rails," Foucault said, a bit testily. Then, realizing he was being unfair, he said, "Cross-country passenger trains. The most recent death was on the Normandie Express. It goes through France, Germany, and a couple other countries, I'm told."

Adele nodded. "And these deaths, the MO was similar?"

Foucault paused for a second, brows knitted. "We're not certain the deaths are murders, actually."

This time, Adele and John did share a look, despite themselves. But just as quickly, their inquisitive glances rebounded back in Foucault's direction.

Adele said, "How did they die then?"

"Heart attacks," Foucault repeated. "Or so it seems. Granted, neither of the victims had a history of heart problems, and one of the victims was quite young. As I've said, two days, two deaths, two trains, two countries..." He made a rolling motion with a finger as if to say *you fill in the blanks.*

"So we're called in just to check it out?"

"First death was in Italy, the second in Northern France," Foucault said. "Check it out is right. We're not sure it's cause for much alarm, and local authorities think it could be a coincidence... But," he paused significantly, his dark eyebrows stretching their confines, "the transportation companies have powerful friends and they want us to hurry this along. *We* want this case investigated and sealed as quickly as possible... It's most likely nothing."

"But," said John and Adele at the same time. This time they didn't share a look.

"But." Foucault nodded. "Just in case, we're sending you two down to where the second train is being held at the station. Make sure. Make it quick. Report back—hear me?"

Adele nodded hesitantly. It sounded routine—throwaway even. And yet, there was something, despite his new twitchy disposition, in the way Foucault was talking that made Adele nervous. He was using the right words, downplaying the murder angle, and yet something about the way he glanced at them, the way he emphasized the two deaths in two countries… Something told Adele there was more to this one than met the eye. She felt a shiver of foreboding stretch down her spine.

"Is that all, sir?" she prompted.

Foucault's eyes flashed for a moment, and he studied her. He opened his mouth, but then closed it again just as quickly and shrugged. "All I know for certain. Rest is up to you." He popped another stick of gum into his mouth, pulling at his collar and muttering, "It's damn hot in here. Out, out! Hurry along." He made twin shooing motions toward John and Adele, bringing the meeting to a close.

CHAPTER FOUR

The painter winced as he dragged the razor across his face, rocking slightly back and forth and swaying in time with the brass jazz pulsing through the bathroom. He hummed to himself as he swayed, stripped completely nude as he examined himself in the mirror. His clothing was folded and placed neatly on top of the toilet lid, a metallic mask resting on the pile just over two black gloves.

The razor moved across one eyebrow, taking away the final remnants of hair. The man hummed along with the saxophone solo pulsing in from the other room and reached for the tape he'd left on the back of the toilet. Still humming, he peeled off a fragment of tape, pressing it to his forehead around the eyebrow and pulling away. He gasped in pleasure at the sheer pain of the sudden removal. He pulled another section of tape and pressed it lower down his face now, over the eye, around the socket. He pulled away again, making sure to catch the final remnants of any fiber of hair from his eyebrow.

Then, staring at the clear, translucent tape, he moved back to the razor, bringing it up to his next eyebrow. He continued to sway, feeling the breeze against his unclothed form in the still, darkened bathroom.

The lights were off throughout most of the house, save the pulsing glare from the small screen he kept by the sink. The screen displayed video image of the apartment where Adele Sharp lived.

The painter glanced down at the apartment again, smiling to himself and humming some more as he reached for the tape again.

"Soon," he murmured softly. "Dear, dear friend, very soon..."

In the background, just above the sound of the pulsing music, he heard the faintest of mewls as if from a cat.

A frown flickered across his face, and he glanced in frustration toward the open door. No rest for the wicked, he supposed. He looked back into the mirror.

Of course, he couldn't introduce himself to Adele *first*. No—best to let a mutual friend make the introductions. First impressions were hard to shake, and he intended to make a marvelous initial approach. He smiled at the thought, staring at the video feed. Someone was exiting the building. He leaned in, peering at the footage from the camera he'd managed to tap into across the street.

"Is that…" The man's eyes narrowed. He recognized that man, wearing a thin white T-shirt and a walrus mustache. He watched as the man left the apartment building, moving up the street and out of sight.

Curious. Was Adele entertaining friends and family? Why hadn't he been invited?

Another mewling sound echoed from down the hall. He gritted his teeth now, not pressing too hard. His teeth, like some of his bones, weren't the strongest things in his body.

He frowned, his face collapsing into a glare as he gazed into the mirror, staring into his deep eye sockets, his bony cheeks etched against thin skin. Not nice to exclude your closest friends… Not nice at all.

He puffed a breath, trying to calm himself, to still the rage suddenly burbling like hot tar from in his chest.

Not nice at all. He'd have to introduce himself soon… Very soon.

The thought of what he had planned for tonight prompted him to relax a bit, sighing in relief.

He ripped the tape away again, wincing in delight at the pain and continuing to hum with the smooth jazz as his naked and bony body continued to sway and dance in the mirror… He trusted his source. Trusted the information.

She'd served food to the agents after all. A cafeteria worker, she'd said. He hadn't known when he'd picked her up late at night across from the DGSI. And yet, he'd struck the jackpot. She'd *known* Adele. Known Adele's friends.

Of course, he'd had her company for more than a week now. He'd only intended to keep her for three days, but after the first escape attempt, followed closely by a second, he'd been required to work a bit harder with the cafeteria worker. Some potter's clay was tougher than others, needed more pressure, more force.

He paused for a moment, some of the moisture from the dampened razor now trickling down his face. He licked his lips and stared into the mirror.

He heard another whimpering sound and this time lost it.

"God damn it!" he screamed at the top of his lungs, slamming his bony hand against the mirror and shattering it. He cursed, glaring now at where blood dripped from his knuckles and speckled the porcelain sink. "Damn it," he repeated, quieter now. The blood poured down his wrist and along his forearm, dripping off his elbow and spattering on the ground, flecking his bare toes.

"Bitch," he muttered to himself, growling through clenched teeth.

He stomped away, leaving his clothing on top of the seat. He marched down the hall, approaching the sealed door with the many locks. The mewling was louder now, more a whimper, really.

"Shut up!" he screamed. "Shut up, shut up!" He flung his hand toward the white painted door, sending a spray of blood from his injured fingers to dapple the doorway itself. He ripped open the bolts, turned the lock, used the final key, and shoved open the door. He jammed his head into the room, like a gopher emerging in daylight, and screamed, "Shut your damned mouth!"

A woman sat strapped to a chair. Shivering, gasping, covered in injures of a different variety. No, none of her injuries had come from glass. He preferred other tools.

The woman's eyes were sealed shut, bloody, her lips could barely move where she gasped, head tilted in the chair.

Seven days of torture had a way of limiting one's awareness.

"Honestly," he said, exhaling now, standing naked in the threshold of the door. "I thought you were already dead."

The woman whimpered again, shaking, trying to cry, it seemed, but failing to emit a full sound.

He sighed, staring at her near corpse. Of course, he'd ruined this canvas. Something about his anger was harder to control when at home. It was easier to manage his emotions when he was out and about. He supposed most people had this issue. Manners were best displayed with new company, and the devil inside often was witnessed by the closest friends.

Not that he considered the cafeteria worker much of a friend. He hadn't even properly spent time with her. He'd ruined some of the intricate patterns. Ripped more than cut in places.

He sighed. "Just die already, will you?" he said. "And in the meantime, shut the hell up."

He slammed the door, whistling now with the saxophone music coming from the kitchen and stomping back in the direction of the bathroom to finish up. She didn't have long for this world. Maybe an hour, tops.

The information she'd provided though... That would last. That had *true* implications for his real friends. For the masterpieces that actually

16

mattered.

He couldn't wait for night to come.

CHAPTER FIVE

Adele and John took his Cadillac lease to the Gare de Rue in Northern France where the Normandie Express had been held.

She regarded John as he exited the vehicle onto the smooth, almost glassy black cement of the parking lot. A stream of passengers moved through the train station, heading in and out in a cavalcade of daily sojourners.

"I hate trains," John muttered as Adele slammed the door and fell into step behind him.

She perked at this sudden interest in conversation. The ride had continued in an impressive stretch of silence, with neither John nor Adele willing to break the ice. Adele hadn't even quibbled with her tall partner about who should drive the vehicle—normally a matter of great contention. Jumping on the chance to hopefully smooth things a bit with her partner, she said, "Oh? What about them?"

"I get sick," John said. "Sick like a dog and puke over everything. Last time, I only had one shirt on a road trip—I stank like vomit for days."

"Lovely," Adele said.

John often said gross or offensive things—it was his way of rattling cages. Now, though, instead of playful, his words felt barbed, as if he were interested in simply offending her for the sake of the offense rather than a shared joke or a playful tease.

Maybe she was simply reading too much into it. Adele sighed, wishing she'd had a chance to go for her usual morning run before her father had arrived, and instead contenting herself with a brisk walk after John's long-legged form in the direction of the large train station built into the flatland of the northern country. Adele acknowledged the tall, curving structure of the station. From within, she could hear the chug of locomotives and the sound of milling passengers.

A local uniform was waiting in front of the station. When he spotted them, the young man glanced at his phone as if double-checking something, and then his expression brightened. He was a round, cherubic-faced fellow, with dimpled cheeks and a thin hairline visible

18

beneath his police officer's hat.

"Hello!" the man called, waving his pudgy fingers in a hyper sort of greeting.

John's eyes narrowed and Adele smiled. Nothing pissed her partner off more than good cheer, and this jolly fellow seemed to have it in spades.

"*Bonjour*," Adele replied. "Are you here for show and tell?"

The man wrinkled his nose for a moment, but then laughed, even though she wasn't sure what at. "Ah, yes, mademoiselle. Agent Sharp and Agent Renee, yes?"

Adele nodded. John just glared.

"Well, come this way, the Normandie Express is sequestered. We transferred the passengers to their destinations, of course," he said, more prattling than advising. As he turned to lead them away, though, Adele coughed, frowning herself now.

"You sent the passengers away?"

The man hesitated, turning back, his double chin pressing against the side of his uniform as he twisted. His dimpled cheeks seemed a bit less pronounced as he cleared his throat. "Umm, yes," he said. "Is that... is that all right?"

Adele shook her head. Friendly and chipper was one thing. Incompetent and people-pleasing was another. Now, she noted, it was John's turn to give a ghost of a smile. This only further darkened her mood.

"Damn it," she said. "What's your name?"

"Oh, ah, yes... I'm Officer Allard."

"Do you have a first name, Officer Allard?"

"Ah, yes. Francis."

"Well," Adele said, testily, "Francis, we're here investigating a potential murder. Sending the passengers home is the same as sending the potential killer home with plenty of time to cook up an alibi, destroy evidence, or simply disappear to the four winds. Do you see why that might be an issue?"

She tried to keep her tone matter-of-fact, but couldn't help the edge creeping in.

If he noted it, Allard didn't seem to mind. "Oh," he said. "Yes, well, that wasn't an option, unfortunately. My captain made sure of that."

Adele sighed. Great. A local cop was already meddling. She shook her head and amended her mood, trying to at least maintain a working relationship. "Thank you for your help, regardless. Well, I suppose it is what it is. Did you at least keep the staff around?"

"Yes, of course!" he said, brightly. "Follow me, please, Agent Sharp and Agent Renee."

Then, with a slight skip to his step despite his heavy frame, the jolly officer led the two grumbling agents into a side service door of the massive train station, and down a long gray hall with thick, edged brick-work.

At last, they reached a white door, which he pushed open. As Adele followed with John and the door hissed, closing on a contained spring system, the train station became suddenly much more muted.

John whistled beneath his breath, pursing his lips and transitioning the expression into one of mild awe. He looked around the high ceilings and the varnished wooden archways. For her part, Adele glanced down, regarding the marble fountain in the center of what was purportedly a train station, and the old-fashioned, wooden ticket-collecting stand with old photographs framed and pinned to the side. She spotted a rest area in one corner, complete with an ottoman and six recliners all facing a sputtering projected screen playing a black-and-white video of some kind.

And the centerpiece of it all, sealed in the strange area, cordoned off from the rest of the train station, was the train itself. Except it didn't look like any train Adele had seen before.

It looked... old, though she knew the Normandie Express was a newer circuit. The train itself had drapes in the windows and a balcony around the front locomotive. Crisp green paint with golden lettering on each of the compartments displayed the name for the company.

Officer Allard, noting their astounded looks, coughed sheepishly and said, "Ah, yes... Part of the deal the Normandie Express made when contributing to the station—an allowance for a private holding area in six of the nineteen stops it makes on its seven-day journey."

"Seven days?" John asked, seemingly even more surprised than before. "Who wants to be trapped on a blasted puke box for seven days?"

Allard chuckled good-naturedly, as if they were sharing a joke rather than listening to a complaint. He turned to Adele as if sensing she were the less prickly of the two agents, or perhaps designating her the senior partner, and said, "Here it is. Would you like to see the crime scene? We've left it mostly as we found it. Without the body of poor

20

Ms. Mayfield, of course."

"Mayfield?" said Adele. "That's not a French name…"

"She came on a boat across the English Channel," the jolly officer said. "A two-week vacation, by the sound of it. I spoke to her son-in-law on the phone. He's agreed to fly in tomorrow and confirm the body."

Adele sighed. This was going to be tricky. Normally, the killers were the ones on the move. This time, the crime scene was. It made routes through at least four countries, and had been traveling for half a day before the murder. The first heart attack had occurred on a separate train line in Italy, but part of Adele—deep down—was hoping they could simply confirm this was an accident and move on. She had other things to worry about back in Paris, and wasn't particularly interested in having to also head over to Italy… though… she did have a friend or two in Bel Paese.

She hid a soft smile at the recollection of Agent Christopher Leoni from *Agenzia Informazioni e Sicurezza Esterna.* The Calvin Klein good looks and immaculate manners mixed with a determination to match her own had made them fast friends.

Adele brought her attention back to the moment. Maybe it wouldn't be the worst thing to have to stay on this particular case for a couple of days.

"Show me where the woman died," Adele said.

Officer Allard nodded, and whistling to himself, he moved past the marble fountain and toward the stationary train. He led them onto the boarding platform, through an open partition in the back of the second car, and into a spacious compartment with chesterfield sofas and blue drapes on the windows.

Adele stepped into the place, impressed John didn't even need to duck beneath the miniature chandeliers dangling from the ceiling.

"Looks smaller from the outside," she said.

Allard cleared his throat. "Ah, yes. Part of the charm, I'm told. Normandie Express promises the charm of a traditional carriage with the luxury of all the modern amenities. I don't know much about trains, but it seems… nice." He shrugged and nodded.

"Nice," grunted John. "Hell with drapes is still hell."

Don't be so dramatic, Adele thought, but didn't say it. Normally, she never would have held back. But as things seemed to have shifted between her and the lanky agent, she didn't want to stir up any more hard feelings, so she let it lie. And for his part, Officer Allard didn't seem to notice John's grumbling.

"Here's where she was found," said Allard, stepping forward and gesturing toward a seat facing the largest window in the compartment.

"On the chair?"

"Well—ah, according to the witness who was here, she was sitting and then jumped up all of a sudden. She died seconds later, sort of draped across the ground and the cushions… like here." Allard gestured with one hand in a sweeping motion.

Adele looked over. "Witness? Someone was here when she died?"

"Oh… Yes? Didn't anyone tell you? Sorry. There was a young woman who'd been here from the start of the trip. A Parisian, in fact. However, she's currently at a nearby hospital being treated for shock."

Adele glanced at John and her partner shrugged back. "Shock?" Adele said.

Allard winced. "She seemed quite upset by the whole experience. Not that I can blame her, of course. It must have been very frightening."

"Well," Adele said, "I can't really do anything here. And no passengers to interview. We'll save the staff for a bit—I think it best we go talk to the young woman. John?"

"Sure," he grunted. "Anything to get us off this contraption."

This time Adele did speak her mind. "It's not even moving," she replied.

Instead of riposting back, John just shrugged and left the train. Adele found her temper rising; it was almost as if he were intentionally trying to make her feel the cold shoulder as much as possible. Well, two could play at that game.

She made to follow her partner, but just then, she heard someone clear their throat and she looked up. There, at the back of the compartment, next to an open door that had a sign which read *Staff Only,* a bald man in a blue and gray uniform, boasting a pointy, pitch-black goatee that reminded her of shoe polish, said, "Excuse me—are you the detective in charge?"

"Agent," she said, pausing, then following with, "Sharp. And you are?"

The man with the goatee glanced at Allard, who quickly said, "Ah, yes—this is the conductor, Mr. Granet."

"Yes, yes," said the man, speaking quickly. He began to move, and

Adele realized everything about him seemed quick, as if he were a human played on double speed. He moved hastily across the car in half the time it might take most and came to a halt in front of her, not gasping, but breathing in a loud, obvious sort of way. She didn't have much time to listen, though, as the sounds of his rapidly spewed words overtook her attention.

"Ah," he said, "Agent Sharp. Look—I'm on a tight schedule. We're a new company, you have to see it our way. Already, we're making headlines—the wrong sorts, I'm sure you understand."

Adele just stood waiting.

His face reddened a bit and he seemed to be resisting the urge to stroke his goatee, instead, doing this strange thing with his hand where he absentmindedly pinched at his neck, squeezing the skin together just about his throat. The skin was quite loose, and for a moment Adele was reminded of a friend she'd once had who'd lost a lot of weight in a short amount of time, causing the skin to be similarly elastic.

"Well," the conductor continued, "now that you've come and seen, is it quite all right if we continue on our way? We'll have to head back to the station. The experience is more pleasure than business and as I'm sure you're aware it's not easy enticing new travelers after such a failed expedition."

Adele blinked in the face of this flood of rapidly communicated words. She winced and said, "I'm sorry Mr. Granet, but until the investigation is over, I can't allow—"

He coughed, cutting her off, his eyes responding to her unfinished sentence with a flash of annoyance. "Come now," he said. "Surely you wouldn't bankrupt us just for some old lady!"

Adele raised an eyebrow and he coughed again, pulling at his neck skin once more. "I mean..." he stammered, "there are so many others who would be missing out."

Adele shook her head. "Sorry, Mr. Granet. The train stays in the station until I say so. Good day."

Then she turned and stepped off the lounging compartment, following John and gesturing for Officer Allard to fall into step

"Which hospital is the witness staying at?" Adele called over her shoulder.

"The General Hospital Ille de France. It's not far."

Adele nodded but didn't reply, thinking about the conductor. He had seemed mighty rushed to get moving, and hadn't seemed particularly bothered by a passenger dying. This didn't point to guilt, but it might point to neglect. As for his desire to keep going, Adele couldn't care less. That wasn't her job. Neglect on either side would allow a guilty party to skate by unnoticed.

It was Adele's job to make sure this didn't happen. First step: interviewing the witness to the death itself.

CHAPTER SIX

The hospital was surprisingly small, no more than two stories, looking more like a converted paper supply company than a medical facility. John and Adele followed Officer Allard into the first floor, through glass doors that didn't slide so much as reluctantly allow themselves to be pushed along a track.

A young woman sat behind a low, dusty counter with peeling varnish strips revealing a plastic frame for what was pretending to be wood. The woman glanced up, peering through her glasses and adjusting a row of pens which she'd stacked neatly on the calendar in front of her. "Can I help you?" she asked, glancing back down at her pens and rolling a couple into somehow preferable positions.

"We're here to see Ms. Dubot," replied Allard. "Is she okay to speak?" He spoke with actual concern in his voice.

The woman smiled as she seemed to recognize Allard, some of her focus shifting now toward the chipper policeman. "Oh, hello!" she said. "How are you?"

Allard leaned against the faux wooden counter, beaming as if he were talking to a long-lost sister. "Wonderful," he said. "How are you doing today, Adrienne? I certainly hope they've cut back your work hours."

Her smile notched up a bit more, as often happens when someone remembers your name. She began to reply, but John stepped in, cleared his throat, and said, "I don't mean to intrude on this little reunion, but could we see Ms. Dubot?"

Adele resisted the urge to roll her eyes at her partner. Allard glanced at John and quickly shook his head. "Reun—no, no, we only just met yesterday. But how about it, is Ms. Dubot up for some company?"

The woman behind the counter had a somewhat cooler gaze as she glanced at John. But then, instead of buzzing an intercom or calling for a nurse, she walked around the counter and began to stroll down the small, simple hallway of the tiny hospital. "Come," she said. "We're understaffed so I'll have to show you. If she's asleep, though, I'm not allowed to let anyone in."

25

Adele waved away the concern and broke into a quick stride next to the receptionist. They passed one room, which had an empty bed against a bare wall. Then reached a second. The woman pushed open the door, a bit of flaking paint spinning to the tiled ground, and then stepped into the hospital room.

This area was cleaner than the first room had been and smelled faintly of cleaning solution and sanitizers.

A slight woman sat upright in a reclining bed, not quite wide enough for anyone besides the small frame of the woman who Adele decided must be Ms. Dubot, seeing as she was the only one wearing a hospital gown in the room.

The woman's eyes widened as the four figures all entered, and she seemed to startle all of a sudden. One frail hand darted up to her chest, but then fell just as quickly as she seemed to recognize the arrivals. "Hello," she said quietly. "You must be the police."

Adele glance at the woman who'd led them here, waiting for a sign of approval, but she didn't receive so much as a nod, so she took the initiative to step further into the room, saying, "Ms. Dubot, hello. We are with DGSI. Do you think you'd be up to answering a couple of questions for us? If anything is too alarming, we can stop at any point you'd like."

The small woman had curling hair and porcelain features, with a slight red flush to her pale skin. The curls seemed natural and bobbed as her head tilted a bit, reclining against the three pillows she'd used to prop herself up.

"Do I have to?" she said. "It was all so horrible."

Adele winced in sympathy but drew nearer to the bed, holding a hand out behind her to indicate the others should remain back.

She stood at a respectful distance, but came to a halt near the foot of the bed. "Ms. Dubot," she said, "we don't mean to take up much of your time. Would you be able to give me a brief recounting of what you saw, though? You don't have to do anything you'd rather not, but it could certainly help if you did."

The woman took a shuddering breath, her eyes still wide in their sockets, as if strained from the inside. She closed her mouth and swallowed, and then, with a quiet murmur, she said, "It was so awful... Her hand... it was cold. She grabbed me..."

Adele frowned. "The victim grabbed you? Were you fighting?"

The young woman shook her head adamantly, her curls shifting and bouncing across her pale face. "No, nothing like that. She wouldn't even talk to me, in fact. I left, but forgot my purse. As I came back, I saw her sitting on the couch, but she looked alert all of a sudden."

"And then?"

"I went to get my purse..." Here Ms. Dubot started breathing heavily, staring off into the distance over Adele's shoulder as if she weren't quite present in the room. "One moment Ms. Mayfield was fine... The next..." A soft sob escaped Dubot's lips.

John and the others had stayed back by the door, following Adele's quiet motions with her hand to stay put. Now, though, Agent Renee broke from the pack and stalked further into the room. The tall agent's shadow cast across the floor and he paused, looking down at the young woman. "Did you know Ms. Mayfield?"

For a moment, Ms. Dubot seemed disoriented as she glanced from Adele to John and back. As her eyes landed on the tall, scarred Frenchman she gave a little gasp and sat up a bit more. Adele hid a smirk. Then Ms. Dubot, covering her reaction, cleared her throat. "No," she said, weakly. "Not at all. I'd never met her before in my life."

"But you were there when she died," John said. "Was anyone else in the room?"

The young woman hesitatingly shook her head. "No one. I didn't see anyone there..."

"Just you and the deceased," John said skeptically.

The woman seemed to be realizing his inference and her eyes widened all of a sudden. "Wait a moment," she protested. "It wasn't like that! Not like that at all!"

"John," Adele murmured, "careful..."

He just shrugged though, and glanced back at Ms. Dubot. "How did she die? In your words."

"If it's not too hard to talk about," Adele said, trying to be a comforting reprieve from the brunt of John's personality.

The woman closed her eyes now, and for a moment seemed as if she might have fallen asleep. Then, her eyes still closed, in a shaky voice, she stammered, "I-I went back for my purse. She was just sitting there, drinking her coffee and looking out the window. Then she suddenly jolted, she gasped and tried to grab my arm as if reaching for help..." The woman winced, but, to Adele's admiration, she pressed on. "Then she fell, jerking a bit, and went still. That's when I screamed and the conductor was brought to the compartment, and the police were called."

After she'd finished, her shoulders slumped a bit, as if she'd just shed some heavy load. Adele nodded in gratitude, and John looked like he wanted to press for more, but couldn't seem to think of what else to ask. "You're sure no one else was in the compartment?" he said at last.

The woman just shook her head, but then opened her mouth to speak. "Not when she died, but... but before, I did see someone pass by. Didn't get a good look at them. And, well, it's a train. A lot of people pass by..." She dwindled off for a moment, and her eyes began to widen. Adele leaned in, hesitant, concerned, and then Ms. Dubot started shaking and trembling, her body jolting.

"Out! Out!" called the receptionist turned nurse. The woman swept into the room, making shooing motions and pressing a red button over the bed, calling, "Dr. Delafosse! Room two! Dr. Delafosee, now!"

The witness continued trembling as if she'd just been dumped into an icy river, and at another angry look from the nurse, Adele and John beat a quiet retreat. A doctor came rushing out of a side room, walking steadily but quickly, passing the agents without so much as a sidelong glance, and then entered into the room, speaking quickly and approaching the patient. "Shock," the doctor was saying. "It's a panic attack, nothing more. Ms. Dubot, you're going to be fine. Can you hear me?"

Then the door was shut and Adele, John, and Allard were left out in the hall. Adele sighed, turning away and glancing up at John. "You didn't have to go so hard," she said, frowning.

John sniffed. "She seemed fine enough. We needed more," he said. "We don't have anything new to go on. For all we know, if it was murder, Ms. Dubot is the guilty party. She was the last to be seen with the victim alive, by her own admission."

Adele resisted the urge to roll her eyes, and was aided in catching the gesture by a sudden ring tone from her pocket.

She fished out her phone and recognized the number. Instantly, some of the acerbity she'd been feeling melted like ice. With a quick glance at John, she began walking up the hall back toward the somewhat-sliding doors to the hospital. Once she was a safe enough distance away, she answered.

"Agent Leoni," she said, smiling and turning to conceal the expression from the two men behind her.

"Adele, how are you?" said the voice on the other end.

In her mind's eye, Adele pictured the Italian agent's perfect jaw line, the superman curl of stray hair resting against his forehead. She pictured his immaculately maintained vehicle and the precision in the way he dressed and acted.

"To what do I owe this pleasure?" she asked.

Normally, Agent Leoni was easygoing enough, but there was an edge to his tone that caused her to perk up as he said, "I hear you're on the other end of the train deaths."

"I was assigned to the case," she said, slowly. "There was one in Italy, too."

"That's why I'm calling. I'm heading up things over here... and I looked into the first death."

"And?"

"I don't believe it was natural," said Agent Leoni in a clipped, somber tone. "Our coroner seems to agree, and is working feverishly to get a toxicology report, but that could take a few days."

Adele's mouth felt dry all of a sudden and she glanced back to where John was pretending not to watch her. She frowned slowly. "We don't have a few days. If this is a serial killer—then they've already struck twice. Only with one day separating them."

"Exactly," said Leoni. "Which is why I'm calling. If I'm right, we don't have a few days for a tox report—the killer will strike again. Most likely tomorrow."

Adele sighed, huffing a breath and shaking her head. "All right," she said at last. "Thanks for the heads-up. We don't have any confirmation on our end of a murder, but we only just got here."

"You do what you think is best, but—"

Adele cut him off. "If you say something is off, then I believe you. What are the odds that two heart attacks on two train lines within two days aren't linked? We'll treat this like a proper investigation. Don't worry. Keep me posted."

"Of course."

"Good luck."

"You too. One other thing," he said. "Victim one was overheard in an argument with the bartender on the LuccaRail the same night he died. We're still looking into it. Obviously, a bandying of words isn't damning evidence, but it is worth noting."

"Thanks, I'll keep my ear to the ground," said Adele.

"And Adele," Leoni said, chuckling in that confident, understated way of his. "It is a pleasure to be working with you again."

Adele tried to suppress the threat of a grin, but failed somewhat. "And you," she said, simply, thinking of the Italian for a moment, remembering how he'd looked, his smile. She shook her head, forcing herself to think of something besides the handsome Italian's jaw line.

After bidding a final farewell, Agent Leoni hung up, leaving Adele standing in the old hospital with a rising sense of uncertainty in her gut. She frowned after a moment, then glanced back at John. Raising her voice, she said, "We need to get a list of all the first-class passengers on the train at the time. Staff as well."

John nodded once. "Who was that?"

"Another agent," she replied, curtly. "From Italy. He's confident this was murder."

Then she turned and exited the hospital, not bothering to look and see if John was following.

CHAPTER SEVEN

Adele paced the small, cramped room back in the Bourthes Precinct, scrolling through the documents on her phone. John sat on the floor, beneath a window, a laptop open on his legs as he also scrolled through the same information.

Adele sighed, but didn't speak. Again, a strange, awkward silence had filled the space between them. By now, it was irritating enough that Adele half felt like addressing it then and there. But what could she say that wouldn't simply make things worse? She shot a sidelong look over at where John continued to stare at his laptop screen, his face illuminated in glowing blue light from the device and also the bright white glare from the naked, tube ceiling bulbs.

As Adele considered what she might say, a staccato knock on the door echoed out in a playful rhythm, then the door opened and a smiling face popped into view.

"Everything all right?" Officer Allard said, glancing from Adele to John in the small space he'd managed to set aside for them back at his precinct.

"Fine, fine," Adele said, forcing a smile. She looked back distractedly at the phone, reading and rereading the names she'd been provided by Normandie Express.

"Anything to drink?" Allard asked.

Adele shook her head, and John just grunted.

"Well... I'll be just out here if you need anything," he said, as if hopeful they might take him up on the offer.

Another shake of the head, another grunt.

The affable agent dipped back out and shut the door again behind him. Something about this brief interlude shifted the atmosphere enough that Adele struck up the courage to glance at her surly partner and murmur, "See anything standing out?"

John kept staring at his screen, frowning. "Joseph Dupuy—the first victim—was a young man in his thirties..."

"I noticed that too."

"I thought both would be old. Pretty rare for a thirty-year-old to have a heart attack."

"What does it say—he was a tech entrepreneur, yes?"

John finally looked up. "You think money is a motive? Bad business venture?"

Adele shrugged. "I'm not ruling anything out. Ms. Mayfield certainly came from wealth. I wonder if she had investments of a type. I'll request that information."

John grunted again, returning to the screen. "Don't know about investments. But it looks like most of her money was inherited from her late husband. She's involved in dog shows and is a breeder."

"Not exactly a tight connection with a tech engineer," Adele murmured. "They're both rich, both were in first-class compartments on their respective trains... but otherwise they couldn't be more different."

John shrugged now, seemingly deciding he had nothing further to add.

For her part, Adele's brow creased into a frown. "Maybe..." she said, slowly, "maybe they knew each other?"

"One was from London, came here on a cruise," said John. "The other was an Italian coder. Doesn't exactly seem like they would have had any reason to connect."

"Well... still worth looking into."

"I guess."

"You guess?"

John shrugged again.

Adele's eyes narrowed. "You know..." she said, testily, "we might not have left things the best, but there's more at stake here than just—"

He cut her off mid-sentence. "You see the staff list?"

Adele gaped at him, hesitant, having been stopped mid-flow. For a moment, she felt like lashing out again, but then she breathed a couple of times, exhaling through her nose, and said, "What about it?"

"Both trains were from the same company. Normandie Express and LuccaRail are funded by Lockport Enterprises."

"I've heard of them before. They're involved with buses and ferries too, if I remember. You don't think they're involved, do you?" Adele's tone softened a bit now that John was actually contributing something.

Her partner shook his head. "Not the company, exactly. But because they're funded by Lockport, they also sometimes share employees. Trade to another line to fill the gaps."

Adele stared. "How do you know that?"

"I wasn't always a helicopter pilot." John grunted. "I did a stint on an overnight ferry for a couple of years when I was a teenager and lied about my age. My point, though, is that I cross-referenced staff names."

Adele stared. "Between the two lines? Anything?"

John nodded once. He held up two fingers. "Two names. Peter Granet, the conductor, and Martin Rodin, the bartender. On Tuesday, they were both in Italy on the LuccaRail, then Wednesday they were on the Normandie Express."

Adele regarded John with a look of surprise. "Good work," she said.

He gave a half shrug.

"So yesterday they switched rails?" said Adele. "Even if that's the case, I don't think Mr. Granet, the conductor, could be involved. He would be at the helm, far from the first-class compartment."

"Unless he took a break," John pointed out.

"Perhaps. But in both deaths? It would be noticed, surely..."

"Well then, that leaves us with Mr. Rodin, the bartender in the dining car. In fact, the dining car is directly next to the lounging area, where Ms. Mayfield was found."

"The bartender you say," Adele said, perking up suddenly. She felt a flutter of excitement in her chest. "Strange you mention him... I didn't ask for a name, but my contact in Italy mentioned the bartender on the LuccaRail was overheard in an argument with the first victim."

John and Adele both shared a look of surprise at this declaration, the tall agent sitting cross-legged, while Adele continued to pace the room, her eyes on her partner.

"So Rodin is our guy?" John asked.

"We can't be sure. But he's the only connection between the two trains. And if he had an argument with the first victim back in Italy, before switching trains for the company, maybe he had motive too. Not to mention," she added, frowning in thought, "he was the bartender, which means he had access to the passengers' drinks."

"They're running a tox report now," John added.

"Exactly. Two heart attacks. Poison would be the obvious murder weapon. And what better way to poison someone than by handling their favorite drink right before consumption?"

John got to his feet, closing the laptop lid and putting it back in the black satchel he'd brought from the car. "Well, Mr. Rodin is our guy then. The staff is all still held back at the train, so our best bet—"

Before he'd finished, though, another quick knock echoed out on the door, and Officer Allard poked his head in again.

"Ah, pardon me," he said, quickly. "But I couldn't help but hearing. You mentioned a Mr. Rodin?"

Adele frowned. "Hang on, were you eavesdropping?"

"Just standing by in case you needed anything," he said, unperturbed by her hostile tone.

John, though, didn't seem to care and instead said, "What about Mr. Rodin?"

"Ah, yes. I'd been waiting to tell you until you were finished in here. But about an hour ago, I received a call from Mr. Granet—the conductor."

Adele frowned now, crossing her arms and facing off across the small, dank room. "And?" she prompted.

"He said Mr. Rodin went missing about an hour ago, after we left the station."

"Missing?" John said. "Did he mention he was leaving to anyone?"

"Not according to the conductor. He vanished. They don't know where he is."

Adele shared a long look with John. "Well," she said. "It's looking worse and worse for our friendly barkeep, isn't it?"

John sighed, rubbing a hand through his slicked hair. "He couldn't have gotten far, could he? He doesn't have his own vehicle."

"Maybe he called a cab," said Adele. "Or maybe he took another train."

"Maybe. Maybe he's still at the station. We'd best start looking unless we want Mr. Rodin to get another shot at some unwitting passenger."

Adele nodded and marched out of the room, speaking over her shoulder, "Let's check any train that's left in the last hour. See if any of the nearby taxi companies were dispatched to the area. And barring that, we search the station, from the top to the basement. No stone unturned. Wherever Mr. Rodin is hiding, we need to find him now."

CHAPTER EIGHT

Adele and John stood before the stationary Normandie Express, glancing at the four other police officers Allard had procured to search for the missing bartender. John's hand braced against the rail of the small balcony at the front of the locomotive as he eyed the police. "Everyone have a picture of the suspect?" he said, his voice booming in the broad station.

The police all regard Allard, who was flashing a printout of Mr. Rodin's face.

"No new trains left in the last hour," John continued, "and a cursory look at the security cameras displayed no one matching Rodin's description leaving the station. Which means he slipped away undetected, or he's still here, hiding inside the station."

The police all nodded in response. Allard then broke them off into groups of two and directed them toward portions of the station for a grid-search pattern. John hopped down from where he'd been standing on the small balcony and approached Adele. "Where do you want to start?" he said.

She thought for a moment. "Maybe the restrooms? Though he might be wanting to blend in."

"Perhaps," said John. "Think he's armed?"

Adele winced. She didn't want to imagine a shootout in a train station full of commuters. "Let's hope not," she murmured.

Then, together, John and Adele moved through the side door which Allard had brought them through and down a tunnel, stepping out into the main portion of the station. This particular train station wasn't the busiest Adele had ever seen. A few people moved about the platforms, some of them clutching bags or tickets, waiting for their rides to arrive.

As she moved along with John, walking briskly to keep up with his long stride, she glanced at the faces of the passengers. A large woman sat on a bench, munching on a sesame bun. A red-haired man leaned against a glass partition advertising a perfume. A family of five gathered around a ticket collector who was standing in front of the compartment to a more modest train when compared to the Normandie

35

Express.

Adele and John passed a small restaurant, with a few customers sitting out on faux patio seating. She scanned the customers, but didn't spot Mr. Rodin.

Her eyes did land on a small pile of books near one of the customers. Her own mind shifted, thinking back to red leather seating in front of a small fireplace. She considered her old friend Robert Henry, and his penchant for books and all things literature. As she thought of him, she closed her eyes for a moment, wishing she'd been able to contact him back at DGSI. She'd need to make another effort soon. Days were passing quickly, where Robert was concerned, and while his health still seemed a bit improved, eventually, if the doctors were to be believed, his case was terminal.

Adele sighed, ripping her gaze away from the small stack of books likely purchased from one of the station stores.

They continued on, still in silence, moving toward a cafe at the back of the station. Adele spotted two of Allard's officers also meandering in the same direction. She watched as one of the officers drew near the cafe, peered through the glass window, and then went stiff.

The officer nudged her partner and pointed. The second officer frowned, his hand darting to his hip holster.

"John," Adele said, slowly. "I think they found something."

John followed her glance and just then, Adele heard shouting. The first officer who'd looked through the glass raised her voice and shouted, "Martin Rodin, hands where I can see them!"

Two firearms leapt into the police officers' hands, now pointing through the reflective glass. Adele cursed and broke into a sprint, with John racing behind her. Adele watched, still racing, as the two officers entered the small cafe.

She gritted her teeth, darting around a family of five, while John bellowed, "Move out of my way!"

She reached the cafe's glass windows a few moments later, her own hand pressed against her holster. Through the smudged glass, she spotted a single customer sitting at a round table, his hands jutting into the air, while the two officers pointed their weapons at his head, shouting instructions.

Adele jostled into the cafe, pushing the glass door with her shoulder and, breathing heavily, coming to a halt inside the room. He was

36

stammering, while the first officer shouted, "Get on the ground! On the ground!"

"What is this?" the man gasped. He had ferret-like features, with an angled face that all seemed to come to a point at the end of a large noise. "Please," he said, "I was just here to speak to a friend—a friend!"

The cafe attendant was leaning over a counter, past the cash register, and shouting, "What are you doing to him! He didn't do anything!"

Adele moved quickly over. She glanced toward the attendant. "Do you know this man?"

The middle-aged woman, who was wearing a green uniform and pinstriped apron, nodded quickly. "Martin. He's a friend. He said he was being sequestered nearby and came by to say hello! What is this?"

Adele looked back toward where Martin was still trying to protest, flustered. She paused, though, watching as one of his hands darted into his pocket. Her eyes narrowed. And then suddenly, Rodin's hand reemerged. He yelled and pulled out a pepper spray, spraying it into the eyes of the two officers.

"Run, Martin!" shouted the woman behind the counter.

Rodin actually paused long enough to blow the older lady a kiss before leaping over the table, slamming his shoulder into John and sprinting out the door.

Adele's stomach twisted as she watched, her own cry of protest dying on her lips as John reeled back, sent tumbling over the nearest table. The woman behind the counter screamed. "Don't touch him! He didn't do anything!"

Meanwhile, the two officers were gasping, thankfully—in Adele's opinion—refraining from firing while blinded. They choked and gagged, their faces covered in pepper spray, their hands wiping through the air.

Adele cursed, running to John's side and dragging him up. As she passed the area where Rodin had been standing, her own eyes began to tear up and she looked hastily away, blinking rapidly and waving at the air before her nose.

"Damn it," she muttered. "John, are you all right?"

Her partner growled, extricating himself from the toppled table and wiping a hand across his eyes.

"Make sure the officers are fine," John snapped, his eyes zeroing in on Martin Rodin's retreating form like a shark spotting a trout. He pushed off the table and broke into a sprint, racing out the door in pursuit of the bartender.

CHAPTER NINE

John's feet pounded the concrete as he slammed through the glass door of the small cafe, his burning eyes fixed on the retreating form of the ferret-faced Mr. Rodin. John cursed, reaching up and wiping in frustration at his eyes. Behind him, as the door slipped shut, he heard Adele, concerned, calling out to the woman behind the counter. "Water, please! I need water for their eyes."

John, though, had his own eyes fixed on a different task.

He raced across the platform, chasing after Mr. Rodin where the bartender ducked behind a newspaper stand.

John called out, "Stop! Rodin—stop running!"

The man glanced back, his angled features rearranged into an expression of fright. He squeaked at the sight of the tall Frenchman barreling down on him and then twisted, turning to race in the direction of the tracks.

John glimpsed a train pulling into the station from the opposite, open-air entrance. The large locomotive hissed and scraped as it whined against the tracks, attempting to bring its girth to a halt. Rodin, for his part yelped and, desperately dodging a row of luggage piled next to the train, vaulted over a suitcase and landed on the very lip of the barrier between the tracks and the passengers.

John doubled his speed, shouting, "Don't be stupid!"

Martin Rodin gave another wild look over his shoulder in John's direction. For a moment, he turned, squeaking, his hand pulling out his small device of pepper spray again.

John's eyes narrowed and his own hand darted to his weapon at his hip. He didn't call out this time, instead favoring to conserve his breath for a lunging sprint across the luggage, bounding over it like a panther, steely muscle and focused fury in Martin Rodin's direction.

The barkeep seemed to make up his mind at the last moment though. With another squeak, he spun around, slamming the spray back in his pocket, and then, with what sounded like an audible gulp, he leapt from the platform just as John reached him.

At the same time, the train pulled into the station fully, coming very

39

close to crushing Rodin.

John cursed, jerking back, careful to avoid the ten tons of steel and metal. The machine chugged past, squealing to a final halt and then resting as a metal barrier. John breathed heavily, staring at where Rodin had managed to just barely reach the other side and desperately clamber his way up and onto the platform there.

Rodin turned around, staring at John through a gap in two of the train cars.

John cursed, glancing up and down, but the train was equally extensive in both directions. Passengers began boarding and disembarking, pouring out into the station and further blocking Rodin from view.

The bartender breathed heavily for a moment, reaching up to wipe a glaze of sweat from his angled features and then paused long enough to give John a coy wink through the small gap between the two train cars.

John's eyes narrowed. And Martin blew a kiss, beginning to turn to dart away again.

Anger began to rise in Renee's chest. He clenched his teeth, narrowing his eyes like a bull at the sight of a red handkerchief. So that's how Martin wanted to play it, was it?

John had seen enough. Going around the train wasn't an option—he'd lose the bastard.

So instead, John, propelled by a rising wave of fury, sprinted directly *toward* the train. Rodin paused, half turned, frowning and glancing back. He watched as John took three sprinting steps with his massive legs and then flung himself at the side of the train.

Rodin's eyes widened and his nostrils flared.

"Yeah, that's right," John muttered beneath his breath. The metal was hot near the wheels and cool toward the top. He pushed off the lower portion of the train coupling, using it to launch his lengthy body upward. His hands snared the slanted aluminum room of the nearest passenger car. His body slipped and his shirt rose, allowing his bare abdomen to press against the cold glass. He realized three women were inside the train car, staring out at him and not quite looking away despite his glare.

John grunted, struggling, and then, kicking, pulled himself onto the roof of the train.

He heard a curse that came from Rodin's direction and didn't hesitate to move. John sprinted across the roof and, spotting Martin now darting toward the nearest exit, he began sprinting along the roof of the train, his massive feet pounding into the metal.

John gasped, his arms swinging like pistons, his legs flashing beneath him. He eyed Rodin's progress out of the corner of his eye, gasping doggedly. And then, as Martin tried to merge into the crowd, angling toward one of the turnstiles, John leapt with a howl.

He dove off the top of the train, colliding with the fleeing bartender.

The two of them struck the ground in a tangle of limbs, both of them gasping and scrambling for supremacy. John was twice the size of the smaller Mr. Rodin, though, and it didn't take long to struggle on top and then grip the man by the collar, hoisting him to his feet.

"No you don't," he snapped, reaching out and ripping the pepper spray out of Rodin's trembling hand.

The bartender slumped now, in John's grip, stuttering and gasping, saying, "I—it was an accident. I didn't—sorry—please don't…"

John snorted and gave a little shake until Rodin quieted. He tested his weight on his ankles, grateful to find his lunge off the roof of the train car hadn't caused any damage. Then he gave Rodin another little shake. "Think that was a smart move, do you?" he asked.

Martin's head hung, and he looked glumly over at John's still watering eyes. John sighed at how miserable the man looked and eased his grip—if only a little. He growled and began to tug at Martin. In the distance, between the trains, he could see where Adele had emerged from the cafeteria and was now watching the two of them, her mouth open, her eyes wide.

John felt a flash of delight she'd witnessed the snare. Just as quickly, though, he hid his expression. He'd hoped things could be smoothed over between them. But she hadn't even been waiting for him outside Foucault's office. He'd seen her enter the building, but then for some reason got off on the second floor. As if perhaps she was trying to avoid him. Then, when she'd entered the Executive's office, her tone had been cool as ice.

Clearly, she still hadn't forgiven him for letting her mother's killer escape.

John sighed at the thought, feeling a twinge of regret. Some things, though, were outside his ability to fix. He looked between the trains at Adele, wishing for a moment that he could just talk to her. Like they used to. Could go back to when things were good between them.

But maybe that would never happen again. Besides, did he really blame her? He'd let her mother's killer escape. He'd thought he'd been doing the right thing at the time, saving the victim. Now, he wasn't so sure. If it meant Adele hated him… was it worth it?

John shook his head, muttering to himself and then pushing Martin Rodin along. He kept a firm grip on Martin's collar and began leading him back around the train, toward one of the crossing bridges. In a growling voice, over the sound of Mr. Rodin's protests, John said, "You have some explaining to do."

CHAPTER TEN

They were back on the train, sitting in the dining compartment with their backs to the glass cabinet full of immaculate china. The long, shining oak table was surrounded by cushioned, antique chairs with beautiful upholstery. Adele sat with her hands clasped, and—at her request—Mr. Rodin had been uncuffed and now sat across from her, hunched in his chair, his angled features and sharp chin all seemingly jutting like knives in John's direction as the tall Frenchman spoke.

"You were told not to leave the train," John growled.

Mr. Rodin snorted, rolling up his sleeves slightly as if against a sudden wave of heat. Beneath, he displayed various tattoos, including one of a small bunny munching on a heart-shaped carrot. The bartender reached up, rubbing absentmindedly at his lower lip, which seemed to have a hole for a piercing, but no lip ring.

"I was told not to leave the station," Rodin said. "My friend owns that cafe, I simply went to say hello. I don't understand why you're treating me like a criminal."

Adele watched John's still red eyes narrow. He pointed a finger at Martin Rodin. "You assaulted *two* police officers."

Rodin winced, but quickly shook his head. "It was an accident, I didn't mean—"

"To spray them with a controlled substance?" Adele asked, quietly. "And did you mean to leave this back at your girlfriend's place?"

"She's not my girlf—" Rodin began petulantly, but then trailed off as Adele plopped a large ziploc bag within a second bag on the table between them. She dusted off her hand and then motioned at the contents. "Speaking of controlled substances..." she said.

John whistled and poked at the bag, causing it to make a sound like a couple of maracas. "That's a lot of pills," he muttered.

"Those aren't mine," Rodin protested.

"That's not what your girlfriend said," Adele countered. "You slipped them behind the counter when you saw the cops coming and then sprayed them to try and escape."

"She's not my girl—"

43

"Focus," Adele snapped. She prodded her finger at the pills, and they again made a shaking sound. The many orange bottles contained within shifted about. "No syringes, I noticed," she said, slowly. "No toxins as far as the police could tell."

He frowned at her. "Toxins? Why would I sell clients toxi—I mean, those aren't mine."

"You're a pill pusher," said Adele. "Is that right?"

"No."

"What better place to deal than in train stations, where you can be on the move long before any police show up."

"I didn't," he declared.

"Martin," Adele said, slowly, leaning in now. "I don't care about the pills. Truly, I don't. I don't even care about you spraying the police."

"Assaulting a federal agent," John added with a growl.

"That's not why I'm here," Adele continued.

Mr. Rodin squeaked, shaking his head and glancing between the two of them. "It's not?"

"No. I'm here because you are one of the only common points between both the LuccaRail and the Normandie…"

At this, Martin Rodin looked actually flummoxed. He raised an eyebrow, then coughed delicately. "What does that have to do with anything?" His eyes narrowed. "I don't know whose those pills are. Why are you treating me like a criminal?"

"Because you are one, aren't you?" John said, never one to mince words or step lightly. The large agent leaned across the table now, pointing a finger toward Rodin's chest. "You were in Italy yesterday, weren't you?"

At this seeming detour in the line of conversation, Rodin frowned. He hesitated, cleared his throat, and said, "I mean… yes. I work for multiple trains. I'm saving up to open my own restaurant." He puffed his chest proudly.

"Look," Adele said, interjecting, "I'll tell it to you straight. We believe foul play was involved in the death of one of your passengers in Italy."

"Foul play? As in *murder*? Hang on a second!" His eyebrows strained the confines of his face, but at last he looked away, out the window toward the marble fountain of the quaint sequestered portion of the larger station. "Impossible. And even if so, what does that have to do with me?"

Adele went quiet, allowing the silence to speak for her and watching his expression closely. But Mr. Rodin was either slow on the uptake or a seasoned poker player, because he betrayed nothing. He simply waited, frowning from Adele to John.

At last, she sighed and said, "Look, Mr. Rodin. You were in Italy and a man died. Now you are here and a woman died early in the morning. None of these," she shook the pills, "are toxins as far as we can tell. But the lab will be checking them. Every single one. Do you see why we might be wanting to speak with you?"

Suddenly, it seemed to dawn on him and his mouth widened in surprise. He began to stammer, tugging at the hole in his lip with one manicured finger, the tattoos on his forearm shifting and then slamming to the table with his arm. "I didn't do anything!" he said. "It's a horrible coincidence. That's all!"

"You had an argument with the first victim," John said, staring out from beneath hooded eyes. "You were overheard."

"I-I..." he stammered, shaking his head. "I don't even remember the man's name."

"Joseph Dupuy," John said, firmly.

"Oh... All right, yes, I remember him. And..." The ferret-faced man trailed off, trying to catch his bearings. At last he sighed and, lowering his voice as if confiding, said, "I did have an argument with him. I remember that. But this man..."

"Mr. Dupuy," said John.

"Right. Mr. Dupuy was angry we didn't stock peach schnapps. That was it. He said it was his favorite and started yelling at me. And... look," he said, slowly, his eyes shifting toward the large bag of pills, then to John and back. "Everything in there... now I'm just guessing, but I *think* everything in there is perfectly harmless. Just a little mood alteration. That's all. Definitely not something that could," he coughed and squeaked, "*kill* anyone. And as for the woman early this morning, she never visited the dining car. Ask anyone. I never served her." He said this last part with a flourish of his tone like someone laying down a trump card. And on top of it, he added, "Besides, why would I kill them? Over a little spat around alcohol? I have worse than that six times a day with most of my customers. You don't tend bar if you're a sensitive sort, I'll tell you that."

Before he could continue, Adele's attention was caught by movement in the back of the room in the direction of the dining car.

45

Allard was standing there with two other officers behind him. They wore white gloves and had empty plastic bags in their hands. Allard was shaking his head.

Adele frowned. She raised her voice. "Find anything?"

Allard said, "Nothing," glancing hesitantly at Mr. Rodin, then back to Adele. "We looked through all the bottles, his room, his belongings… No poisons of any kind. Coroner gave a preliminary report of the pictures we sent of the pills and labels. Some Vicodin, a few Adderall—nothing dangerous."

"You went through my things?" Mr. Rodin said, his voice rising.

"You knocked me over after dousing everyone with pepper spray," John returned. "Call us even or take it up with the company." John looked to Adele, and she volleyed the glance back to Allard, who shrugged helplessly again.

Adele returned her attention to Rodin, considering his words. A brief argument at a bar wasn't unheard of. And though they'd been informed there'd been words, no one had been able to verify *what* the argument had been about. Right now, all she had to go on was Rodin's own testimony. Not only that, but the death of Ms. Mayfield had occurred early in the morning, only a few hours after the train had departed. Someone like Mayfield likely wouldn't be visiting a bar so early, which meant Rodin was likely telling the truth—he'd never even served her. Plus, if the pills on him were mild at best… where did that leave them? Ms. Mayfield didn't seem the sort to take up with some pill pusher, either. This, coupled with the failed search, didn't sit well with Adele.

"Mr. Rodin… I don't know what to make of you," she murmured. "You assaulted police officers, ran from a federal agent, have more than one controlled substance, and are sitting across from me lying through your teeth. Why should I believe you?"

Martin stared back, blinking and shaking his head. "I… I—I didn't kill anyone. I didn't!"

Adele sighed. She stared at Mr. Rodin, reading him, trying to find a crack in the facade. But while he struck her as a bit of a rat, he didn't seem the killing sort. Too squirrelly, too scared. But then again, looks could be deceiving.

"Hang on," he quickly interjected, eyebrows rising. "What time?"

"Excuse me?"

"What time did this woman die? When exactly?"

"It's hard to say *exactly*," Adele countered, "but probably around nine a.m. Why?"

"Because," he said, breathing a sudden sigh of relief and leaning back in his chair, "I was with a," he coughed, "client from eight until nine. *Not* Ms. Mayfield. A client in the dormitory car. A Mr. Steter. He works in the dining car with me and purchased a *decent* amount of," he coughed again, "merchandise."

"What sort of merchandise?" Adele pressed.

But at this Rodin looked pointedly away from the pills and shrugged. "Things and stuff," he muttered. "Just ask Mr. Steter. Johnny. I was with him all morning. He took a damned time picking out his usual supply, I might add."

Adele shared a look with John, who shrugged. "We'll be checking up on that," she said, directing the comment toward Mr. Rodin.

"I'm counting on it," he countered, a new confidence in his tone, carried by a swell of relief. "I never even saw the old lady who died. Ask *anyone.* No one will have even seen me near the first-class compartment. I was in the dormitory car all morning. There were at least two other valets there as well. Just ask around. It'll check out."

"It better," John said.

"It will," Rodin insisted.

Adele massaged the bridge of her nose, then glanced at Allard. "Think you can double-check his story?"

The cheerful policeman nodded a couple of times. "Of course. We need to take him in anyway," he added, wincing sympathetically toward Rodin. "You know for all the…" He mimed a spraying gesture and tipped his head toward the pills.

Adele paused for a moment, thinking, glancing back at Rodin, who'd gone rigid again at Allard's words. But then she sighed and made a shooing motion. "He's all yours," she said. "Just tell me if his alibi fails to check out."

"You got it!" Allard said, happily. "And, umm, Martin, if you don't mind, please come with us." The policeman stood in front of the other officers, gesturing politely at Rodin.

For a moment, Adele thought he might make a break for it. But then the weasel-faced man sighed. Rodin didn't say anything as he pushed away from the table, got stiffly to his feet, and marched indignantly away from the agents, toward where Allard and a pair of handcuffs stood waiting.

As Rodin was cuffed and one of the officers came over to retrieve the bag of pills and follow Allard off the train, Adele leaned back, glancing up at the ceiling again.

"Think it'll check out?" she murmured.

John looked over. "His alibi? Dunno. Nothing toxic on him. Except maybe his personality."

"Right. I was worried you'd say that. I... I don't think he's our guy."

"You sure?"

"Pretty damn. I mean, if he was lying about being in the dormitory car..."

"Think he was?"

Adele shook her head. "You?"

John shook his as well.

Then, in near synchronization, they both emitted belly sighs and stared out the window. As they sat in silence, Adele felt a sudden shiver along her arms. She closed her eyes, staving off a rising tide of anxiety all of a sudden. Something just felt off about the case... She remembered the same sense she'd gotten from Executive Foucault. He'd been cagey, strange... But the sense of foreboding she'd felt around him had been *different* than usual.

Or maybe he'd simply tried to quit smoking and it had affected his mood. Now, Adele had the same sense... Something was off— something didn't sit right. But what? Had Rodin been lying? She didn't think so. He seemed a coward—a low-level pill pusher. He'd had *pepper spray* as his weapon of choice. A hardened killer would certainly have had a better out, wouldn't they have? And the way he'd claimed he'd been in the dormitory car, the sheer expression of relief... She didn't think he was lying. Allard would have to confirm it...

But if Rodin wasn't the killer, then who was?

CHAPTER ELEVEN

Night had fallen, and through the thin glass sunroofs of the sequestered part of the station, Adele glimpsed moonlight brushing the windows. She sat in the lounge car of the train, staring up and out of the window where she reclined in the chesterfield.

Her phone sat on the table in front of her, the speaker squawking as she listened to Foucault, his instructions uttered brisk and clear.

"I'm sorry, Agent Sharp, but there is no alternative," he said. "We are under immense pressure from the train company to allow them to embark again. We can't keep them stationary any longer."

Adele exhaled through her nose. "Bureaucrats already involved?"

"Of course."

"They realize we probably have a serial killer on our hands, don't they?"

If a tone could sound like a shrug, Foucault's did. He said, "I'm not sure they're looking too closely at that. The train has lost tens of thousands of euros just sitting still like it has. I suspect the cost of any further layover is being weighed. This Mr. Rodin—did his alibi check out?"

Adele exhaled deeply, nodding, then realizing he couldn't see, she said, "Yeah. Allard called before I called you. Martin Rodin was in the dormitory car all morning. Three separate witnesses. No way he touched Ms. Mayfield…"

"I'm sorry to hear it."

Adele frowned in frustration. "So what then? We continue investigating from back at headquarters? A moving crime scene is hard to track. Moving passengers and staff notwithstanding, our suspects will be on the move."

"Yes, well, I thought about that, Agent Sharp. One of you needs to stay with the train."

Adele flinched. She glanced over her shoulder now, across the car to where John Renee was now reclined against the couch furthest from her, his eyes closed, his arms over his chest as he breathed heavily.

"One of us?" she said.

49

"We don't have the funds for both, and the company refuses to discount. They already think we've cost them enough as it is."

"Your bureaucrats? Are they no help?"

"They've set aside one sleeper car. Either Renee or you will stay on. I know my pick."

Adele waited, but Foucault didn't provide this information. She considered the case, and glanced out toward the station's skylights again, her eyes drinking in the reflection of the moon. Still early in the night, but plenty more time for another victim to fall. Plenty of time for the killer to strike.

But she also thought of Paris, thought of her mother's killer, loose and about. She wanted to hunt that bastard, but she knew if she left, then no one would remain behind on behalf of the passengers...

Not only that...

But as she sat there, the same feeling of foreboding she'd sensed back in Foucault's office, and again in the lounge car—it filled, rising like a tide in her chest and threatening to cut off her breath.

She exhaled slowly, trying to place the source of the emotion. She was talking to Foucault again, but was now starting to wonder if perhaps her sense was coming from internally. Maybe she'd misread the Executive... She couldn't quite place the feeling, but it clawed and cloyed at her chest.

She glanced over to where John was still napping on the couch furthest from her. Perhaps it was good they were separated for now. Things hadn't gone back to the same. Perhaps they never would.

She wasn't sure she could allow John to take the case over... It wasn't that she didn't trust him to solve it, but the last time she'd left a case in his hands, a killer had escaped. Perhaps it wasn't fair to think like that, but Adele had a job to do—lives were on the line. Then again, if she stayed, then who would find her mother's killer?

She thought of Ms. Mayfield, of Mr. Dupuy. Two victims, two trains, two countries...

And again, the same clawing sensation of deepest foreboding...

"I'll stay," she said at last. "Sleeper car, you say?"

"Not much to look at—certainly not first class. But it should suffice."

"I'm sure I'll be fine," she said, sighing. "I guess there's no chance at going for a morning jog on a train."

"I hear they have a gym. Are you certain, Adele? I'm sure Agent

50

Renee wouldn't mind—"

"I'm fine, sir. I don't need any more time off. I'll stay."

"Well, good luck. And Adele, be careful... As you're aware, the worst part about a killer you don't see is if they see you. And on a train, in such close quarters, there won't be the protection of other agents, of places to run, to hide, to call backup. You'll be on your own until we can stop the train and send help. It'll be different protocol than you're used to."

"Got it," she said. "If the killer knows I'm trying to find him, and if he's here, he'll take a shot at me. I expect it, sir."

"Just so long as you're aware. Good night, Adele."

"Yes sir. You too."

***

She listened to the quiet chug of the train as it moved through the night, finally released from its station and allowed back on its merry way in the North of France as it continued toward Germany. She twisted, remembering in her mind's eye the look of hurt on John's face when she'd woken him and told him she'd be working this one alone. That Foucault wanted him back.

Hurt. Such a strange thing for him to express, almost as if he'd taken it as some sort of rejection. But hadn't that been the tenor between them recently? Hadn't they been going cold? Not just their friendship... but everything.

Still, John hadn't seemed to want to leave and when he had, he'd stomped off, leaving the train without so much as a goodbye.

She twisted and turned in the small, cramped room in the sleeper car. Certainly not first class, and according to the Executive, this sleeper was normally reserved for staff. She'd been in prison cells with nicer cots. Her back ached, and her foot tingled from a frigid draft gusting through a window that refused to fully close. The rush of air through the small gap made a soft whistling noise like a tea kettle and twice Adele had resisted the urge to punch the glass.

She twisted again, sitting up at last, her feet dangling over the cramped space toward the floorboards.

She heard a creak.

Adele froze, staring toward her door. For a moment, she glimpsed a flash of light, as if from a flashlight beneath her door frame. She didn't

51

hear anything. Someone had stopped outside her compartment. Her hand darted toward her nightstand where she kept her weapon. She held the comforting, cold metal in one hand.

The light remained... She thought she could hear someone breathing.

A second later, though, it passed by, disappearing.

Frowning, Adele got to her feet, gripping her weapon and holding it behind her back. She pushed open the door and glanced up and down the hall.

No one in sight. Four other doors in this sleeper car, all cramped together.

She waited, looking for another flash of light. But none came. Maybe one of the other passengers had taken a bathroom break?

Or maybe...

Had the killer come by? Looking for her?

She closed her door again, her feet cold against the wooden floorboards, and eased back on the rough cot, careful not to throw herself too hard against it, as the cushions alone would do little to protect her back.

She reclined against the poor excuse for a pillow, staring up at an overhead luggage compartment.

No one in the hall, like a ghost. But ghosts weren't real.

What if the deaths really were natural causes, and they were hunting ghosts in the night? What if she was making things too personal...? She could feel this *need* to catch the bad guy. A need to not let him get away again.

Again?

Again. She frowned at the thought. Her mother's killer had escaped John. She didn't want the same thing to happen here. Ghosts in the night... Maybe they were all fooling themselves...

And yet she couldn't shake the deepest, prickling sense of foreboding. It came rushing back like the wind through the window, and Adele closed her eyes, trembling, trying to fall asleep in the face of a mountain of certainty that something was about to go horribly wrong.

CHAPTER TWELVE

He stood as still as one of the statues in the garden, eyes fixed on the large mansion beyond the black gate. He admired the marble pieces tastefully arranged amidst the hedges and porcelain fountains. One of the statues had a faux-chryselephantine quality to it, though the gold and the ivory seemed faded with weather, suggesting a replica. He had statues of his own. But he'd always preferred paintings.

Now, though, he was in search of a masterpiece of a different variety. He watched the house from his parked car, his thin, bony frame wrapped in two sweaters against the cool of night. Even with the heat on, he shivered, his one good eye closing for a moment against the drying effect of the vents.

A figure moved in the downstairs study, by the two red leather chairs. The fireplace was going, but the figure moved slowly now, pausing once to put out a bracing hand and cough at the ground.

The painter considered the fellow inside, wincing in sympathy. A bad cough, it seemed. Over the last week, as he'd watched, careful to get to know his new friend, he'd noticed Robert beginning to move slower and slower.

Whatever ailed him was having its way.

The painter allowed himself an easy smile, his gaunt features twisting in the dark of his car. Soon, the sickness would be the least of Robert Henry's worries.

The painter reached out, unlocking his car and checking for his black satchel in the back seat. He wore leather gloves and besides the two hoodies, he'd gone through the ritual of shaving his head, his eyebrows, his arms, even his nose. No DNA evidence left behind. He would even wear a mask—not to disguise his face, but to prevent spittle or saliva from landing anywhere compromising.

Sometimes his friends struggled.

As he pushed open the unlocked door, his eyes still fixed on Robert Henry's coughing form in the lower study, he paused for a moment, simply admiring the scene. Sometimes, beholding art was reward in itself.

Robert coughed again, leaning against the table by one of his red leather chairs. He frowned, staring down at the piece of paper he'd left on the table. The inkwell and pen sat open next to his calligraphy kit. Adele had once teased him about it and he found it fitting he write this final letter—this gift to her—in the same ink.

He smiled softly to himself, leaning back now in the red leather chair closest to the window, facing the second chair—the one Adele had often frequented when she had a chance to visit. Robert murmured to himself as he reread the letter, his eyes tracing the cursive loops and the perfectly executed lettering across the old, yellowed paper. He'd taken the paper from one of the first journals he'd bought as a boy.

Robert smiled again, leaning back and glancing toward where the rest of the journal—mostly unused in his youth—lay resting on the table, beneath the ink well.

Would Adele appreciate the gift?

He wondered... For a moment, at the thought, a flash of frustration jolted through him. He sighed and closed his eyes, staving off the sudden bout of despair. It was getting worse as the days progressed, harder to think straight. To think like himself.

He missed Adele. Missed her dearly. But where he was now going, she couldn't follow. Not yet. Hopefully not for a long time.

Which brought him back to the letter.

He paused, picking up the pen and pushing it against the bottom of the paper, and then, with careful, smooth strokes, he signed the letter, nodding and smiling to himself as he did. He folded the paper, placing it in an envelope upon which he wrote, again in cursive, *To My Dearest Adele Sharp.* Then he licked the envelope, sealed it, and placed it, with a trembling hand, between the pages of the small yellow-papered journal.

***

The painter went still, frowning, glancing over his shoulder and through the back window.

Two bright lights flashed in his rearview mirror, and he gritted his teeth. A neighbor? A delivery driver?

A figure got out of the car and began to move up the sidewalk.

The painter hesitated, his frown deepening. He turned his head, following the progress of the figure up the sidewalk. Hot air streamed from the vents against his chin and the side of his neck. The man in question was solidly built, wearing a single white T-shirt despite the cool air. He also had a thick, drooping mustache.

He recognized the man... not just because of Elise, his masterpiece, or even Adele—his dearest friend. Not even because of the grainy image from the security footage earlier that morning. But they'd met, once, nearly five years ago.

The painter frowned at the memory. He'd gotten close then, very close.

What was he doing here, though?

The painter watched as Sergeant Sharp moved through the black gate, past the statuary in the garden and up the steps to the manor. A deep booming sound echoed out from where he knocked on the door.

A second later, from his vantage point, the man watched as Robert readjusted himself, pulling a bathrobe across his dwindling form and limping through the study toward a side door that led to the hall.

Robert's front door swung open a moment later, washing the garden and the front steps with bright orange light. Sergeant Sharp said something, which the painter couldn't hear, and Robert smiled, gesturing for him to enter. A moment later, the door closed, leaving the painter out in the dark.

His friend was inside, entertaining another guest.

Could he have two friends tonight?

He dabbed thoughtfully at one of his shaved eyebrows. Then he shook his head. No... Two was too many. Especially if one of them was a man like Sergeant Sharp. He carried his physique like someone who knew how to take care of himself.

Not a problem, given proper preparations. The painter had spent his fair share of time creating art with the muscle-bound and mademoiselles alike. But he didn't have the proper sedatives for Sergeant Sharp. No... not tonight then.

The painter sighed in frustration. He'd gotten rid of the cafeteria worker he'd picked up as she'd finally faded earlier in the evening. That particular piece hadn't turned out how he'd imagined. Now, though, he had nothing to play with tonight. No canvas, no paints, nothing...

Grumbling to himself, he twisted the key and pulled away from the curb, swerving back up the road and leaving Robert Henry's house behind. For now.

CHAPTER THIRTEEN

"Nice place," Joseph Sharp said, glancing around the entrance to the mansion. The carpet alone looked like it might cost more than his mortgage. "So you're Robert?" he said, finally, his eyes landing on the small man in a silk bathrobe.

The fellow in question had immaculate hair, as if he'd only just combed it into place, an effect betrayed only by the glossy sheen, suggesting a copious amount of product. The man before him had a small, perfectly maintained mustache and eyes that carried a hidden weight of kindness.

"I am," said the man and then he winced, coughing into his fist and holding out an apologetic hand.

"Sounds bad," said the Sergeant.

"Hit my lungs about a week ago," said Robert. "Not much longer now."

Joseph nodded curtly. "I'll keep you in my prayers."

"I'd like that."

They stood awkwardly in the entryway for a moment, the Sergeant glancing around at some of the paintings tastefully lining the hall. He didn't have much patience for paintings. A whole lot of money just for pieces of colored paper as far as he saw it.

He glanced toward the open door to their left, which seemed to lead into a study, with books on shelves and two red leather chairs facing a fireplace.

"Would you like to come sit?" said Robert.

The Sergeant shook his head. "Can't stay long. I'm leaving to return to Germany early tomorrow."

"Ah, of course. No worries. Well, then, I of course recognize you, Mr. Sharp. How can I be of service?"

"Well... I don't know much about service. I heard from my daughter your health was declining. Sorry."

"It's quite all right. I've made my peace." He smiled again. "It's funny how many things used to worry me that now seem so silly."

"I know what you mean," said the Sergeant, his tone unwavering, his eyes fixed and gaze firm. He felt a flutter of emotion in his chest, but didn't quite know what to do with it, so he returned his attention to the small Frenchman. "Your English is really good," he said.

"Thank you. So is yours."

"I... I just wanted to stop by... And—" The Sergeant scratched the back of his head, glancing toward the two red leather chairs in the study.

Robert waited patiently, his small arms folded over his chest, the silk of his bathrobe crinkling in folds, suggesting it was a few sizes too large now.

"Elise will make good company, you know," the Sergeant said gruffly, clearing his throat. "When... well, when you kick it."

"Kick it?" Henry said, raising an amused eyebrow.

"You know. When you..."

"Die?"

"Yeah. Put in a good word with Elise, could you?" the Sergeant said, reaching out and patting Henry awkwardly on the arm, then withdrawing his hand.

"Ah, the afterlife?"

"Yes," said the Sergeant entirely unapologetically. "Heaven. If you make it, I'm sure she'll show you around. Elise was nice like that."

"Your daughter must have picked up that trait from her."

The Sergeant hesitated. For a moment, he wondered if Robert was taking a passive-aggressive shot, but the small man was still smiling, and he didn't seem the sort at first blush. At last, the Sergeant sighed and said, "You've been good to my daughter... I just wanted to come by and say... well, that. Since, well, I might not be able to again. I've always meant to thank you."

"Thank me for what?"

The Sergeant felt a spurt of anger, and he wasn't quite sure why. But he shrugged and shook his head, like a grizzly dislodging droplets from its fur. "Look—Adele and I don't always see things the same way. She's a good girl. She needed someone like you, a mentor."

"You raised an amazing child. That credit goes to you."

"Mostly her mother, really."

"I wouldn't be so sure," Robert said, smiling. "You both have the same eyes. Same grit."

The Sergeant paused, feeling a flicker of emotion in his chest. The man's words—a man he'd just met—shouldn't matter so much, should they? And yet still, he felt for a moment like he'd just been given a gift. The Sergeant sighed, then said, "Maybe you're right. I tried. I really did."

"I believe you," said Robert with a gentle nod. "I... Speaking of Adele, there's something I wanted to give her, but I'm just..." He shook his head.

"You can give it to her yourself," the Sergeant said. "Whatever it is."

"I'd like to. But I think she's out on a case and," Robert swallowed, breathing shallowly a moment to stave off another bout of coughing. "If I'm honest, I don't know how much longer I have."

The Sergeant glanced at the frail man. "You look sick, but not *that* sick. You can hang on a few more days, no?"

Robert chuckled for a moment, shaking his head and muttering beneath his breath.

"What was that?" the Sergeant asked.

"Oh... nothing. Just... Yes, you two are more alike than you know." He sighed now, and shrugged. "Maybe you're right. I'll just give it to her myself, I think. I... Well..." He frowned now, shaking his head slowly. "It's the funniest thing. But I have this feeling... you know... Like I might not see her again."

The Sergeant waved his hand airily. "Ah, forget about it. You'll see her. Buck up—she'll stop by as soon as she's back. I'm sure she will. I know at least that about my daughter. She's a loyal sort. A bit emotional at times, but loyal."

Robert nodded. "Yes, she is that. Well, you've convinced me. I'll hang on to it until I see her in person. Thank you, Joseph."

The Sergeant coughed hesitantly and shrugged his large shoulders. "Well... Good then. And—yes, thank *you*. For who you've been to her."

The Sergeant jutted out a hand. Robert reached to take it, but began coughing again and doubled over.

Joseph looked at the old, frail man and sighed. He'd seen so much death that now it almost seemed par for the course. He remembered as a child, how invincible he'd felt, how often he'd simply refused to contemplate what came next...

The Sergeant kept his hand extended, and Robert finally manage to recover, grip it, and murmur in a quiet, strained voice, "The pleasure was mine. Truly. And if what you say is true, Mr. Sharp, I'll tell Elise you're thinking of her."

"Appreciated."

Then, without further ado, Joseph Sharp turned and pushed out the door, frowning. He wasn't sure what sort of man Robert really was. But Adele often had a nose for charlatans, and Robert didn't seem the sort. Even on the verge of death, he offered an attempt at placation. A gift to the Sergeant. And a gift to Adele. He could see in Robert's eyes he wasn't so sure about eternity, or anything that lay beyond. But in Joseph Sharp's opinion, oblivion or otherwise, he'd see his wife again.

That was a matter of fact.

He nodded to himself, giving a half wave as Robert called in farewell, and then marched down the steps, leaving the mansion behind him and heading back toward his waiting taxi.

CHAPTER FOURTEEN

Adele stood in the dining car, one hand braced against the lacquered counter of the bar, her eyes fixed on the station ahead of them. She felt the train chugging along, the French countryside flitting by as the Normandie Express dipped east of Paris, nearing the German border.

No murders in the night. She had the staff check rooms. Everyone alive and accounted for.

Had they been wrong about this whole enterprise? A murder per day, though, meant *today* would be the next kill.

Adele frowned as the train began to squeal against the tracks, coming to a halt in the last station before the German border.

She looked through the windows, still standing and swaying with the motion of the sudden stop. A voice announced over speakers, disguised beneath one of the chandeliers, *"Last stop for day passengers. We plan to remain for no more than half an hour. Be back by ten for the next leg."*

Adele pressed forward now, her forehead practically pushed against the glass as she watched passengers arrive and board the train, gathering before the two separate entrances. The first, near coach, she ignored.

Her eyes were drawn to the small gathering of first-class passengers now waiting for one of the ticket collectors to wave them aboard.

Her breath fogged up the glass as she leaned in, eyes narrowed, watching the new passengers. She witnessed a middle-aged couple board first; a smiling woman and a stern-faced man handed their tickets to the attendee. They were quickly ushered aboard, along with one of the valets who carried their luggage.

Another one of the valets waited, watching expectantly for the signal from the ticket collector that he should grab the luggage.

The passengers idled by, waiting for the permission to start boarding. Adele sighed, still watching, her breath steaming the glass. As she stood, she thought back to Paris, back to her apartment. She felt a flash of guilt at having left her father alone after making him fly from Germany. She'd needed to tell him everything in person—but the

61

timing of this new case hadn't been ideal... Maybe she owed him a call.

She kept her eyes fixed on the passengers as they also waited, watching the ticket collector. As she did, she reluctantly reached into her pocket, pulling out her phone. She swallowed, lifting the device. For a moment, she paused, but then, instead of calling her father, she dialed Robert's number from heart. So many times, in the middle of a case, she'd had to contact her old mentor. He was a well of information, a crack detective, but even more than that: a dear, dear friend.

She waited, listening as the phone rang. Her stomach twisted a bit as unease settled on her. "Come on, Robert," she murmured.

No answer. She waited for the automated voice and then after the beep said, "Hello, Robert. I'm sorry I haven't called. Busy with the case. Just... I imagine you're in treatment or something. When you get the chance, if you could... please shoot me a message or something. I'll come to see you first chance I get after the case. Have a good day."

She lingered for a moment, still holding the phone, wondering what else to add, but then just hung up. Anything else could be said in person.

The phone didn't stay lowered, though. Now, she did call her father, his name stored in her device only as The Sergeant.

The phone began to ring and her father picked up quickly.

"Adele?" he said.

"Hey," she replied. "Hey, sorry. I just had a moment here. Was wondering how you are."

"Fine. You?"

"I'm—I'm fine. Look, I'm sorry for just leaving you. I'll be back from the case as soon as possible. Like I said before, make yourself comfortable at the apartment. If you'd like—"

"Don't worry about it," the Sergeant said. "I'm heading home anyway."

Adele swallowed. "When?"

"Tonight."

"Oh. You sure? You don't have to. You're welcome to—"

"I'm sure. Look, sorry, Adele, my taxi is here. Have a good day."

"Goodbye..."

This time, the Sergeant hung up and Adele slowly lowered her own phone. She continued to stare through the glass at the milling passengers, some of them growing impatient in the interim. She glanced at the phone, wondering if she should have insisted he stay. But her father was a decisive man. If he wanted to leave, then he wanted to leave. Nothing she could do…

She felt the stirrings of disgruntlement, but forced herself once again to stare through the glass and fixate on the passengers nearest the front.

There were only about six first-class passengers joining them for this next leg of the trip. One man in particular stood out to her. Not so much because of his appearance, but because of the way the other passengers had given him a wider birth. Perhaps he smelled. But as Adele watched, she glimpsed a surly, frowning expression across the man's face. He had no facial hair, and a dark shock of fading hairline that was clearly dyed. The man's eyes stretched in folded frown lines, and his lower lip seemed to be permanently jutting forward as if he tasted something sour.

As the surly man regarded the other passengers around him, the source of the sour taste seemed to become evident, as his scowl only deepened near other humans.

One of the valets reached out, nodding politely, and tried to grab the man's bag, but the angry man suddenly shouted. Even from within, through the glass, Adele heard the words, "Get your dirty paws off," followed by a dark muttering, "Stupid bastard."

The man with the dyed, receding hairline glared at the valet until the young man retreated, apologizing profusely, his face red.

A few of the other first-class passengers looked on in disapproval, but instead of quelling his behavior, the surly man turned on them and demanded, "What? Mind your own damned business." And then, jamming a crumpled ticket hard into the hand of the collector, he pushed past, entering the train.

Adele noted the way he protectively gripped the brown satchel the bellhop had tried to grab. Curious.

But there had been no murders in the night. Which meant what? Was she just looking for a needle in a haystack? Trying to find someone to blame?

Maybe they had gone about this the wrong way. Maybe the murders weren't tied to days, but trains. Maybe the murderer had to move to another train before he killed again. Or, perhaps, not the trains, but the countries. A death in Italy, one in France, and the next one?

Adele bit her lip. They were at the last stop before the German border. What if the killer was waiting for them to enter? She watched the old, surly man clutching his brown bag as he disappeared behind the ticket collector into the first-class compartment.

Adele's countenance darkened a bit, but as she peered through the window, toward the passengers, she recognized a different face. Her eyes went wide, and her lips formed a sudden smile. This face was much friendlier and handsomer than the one prior.

Her breath suddenly fogged the glass a second time, and for a moment, she wasn't sure why she couldn't see, but then quickly, feeling embarrassed, her cheeks heating up, she reached up and wiped hurriedly at the misted surface.

The person in question spotted her also, it seemed, and was now waving in a good-natured, easygoing sort of way. She tried to suppress a grin and waved back before pushing away from the lacquered counter and moving quickly through the car toward one of the entrances.

Adele brushed past one of the valets, who was lugging a particularly large suitcase aboard, and smiled down toward where Agent Leoni from Italy was now handing his ticket to the collector.

She waited expectantly as the ticket collector nodded, ripped off the top of the paper, and handed the stub back. Christopher Leoni was wearing plain clothes and even carried a suitcase. He took the two metal steps up to the back entrance of the train and entered past Adele.

"It's good to see you," he said, winking.

As he brushed past her, she detected the faint odor of cologne. His hair was as she remembered, perfectly set, with a single curl errant from the rest dangling over his forehead. His features were handsome in a clean, expected sort of way. Movie star good looks, she'd thought before. In the past she had characterized John as a James Bond villain, but if so, then Agent Leoni was much like James Bond himself. Not to mention, he'd once helped pilot a plane on an open highway in Germany, and helped her save a life in the process.

"What are you doing here?" she said, moving along with Leoni away from the ticket collector and the other first-class passengers toward one of the sleeper cars.

He glanced over his shoulder, as if making sure no one was listening in, and then said, beneath his breath, "I managed to talk to one of my superiors and show him the merit of my theory."

Adele's eyebrows rose. "So we're both still thinking murder?"

"I'm certain of it," he said. "You look lovely as ever, by the way."

He grinned.

Adele pressed her lips, trying to hide her smile. "Oh? You too." She chuckled. "Not to be a bore, but did you get the toxicology report back?"

The Italian agent shook his head. "Not yet. But I know that when we do, it will confirm what I think."

"How do you know?"

Leoni said, "Thirty-year-olds don't die of heart attacks. Not one day before someone else dies in a similar way. Call it a hunch, call it instinct. I seem to remember you went off that quite a bit last time we worked together." He gave a good-natured chuckle, which she returned.

The two of them had come to a halt outside an open door to one of the first-class sleepers. Adele glanced in and felt a jolt of jealousy. In a forlorn way, she said, "That's like three times the size of my room."

"The benefits of being an Italian," he replied with a wiggle of his eyebrows. He stepped in, pushing his suitcase into the spacious compartment beneath the bed.

Adele stood in the doorway, then glanced over her shoulder and watched as another couple began moving down the car toward another open door.

"It'll be good to have the backup," she said quietly, "but if you're right, there was no death last night... which means..."

"A murder every day," said Leoni. "I would've been surprised if they struck *twice* yesterday. If they kill again, it'll be today."

"Maybe... I was thinking it could be a murderer in each country."

The Italian winced. "Either way, we're nearing the German border. The killer will strike again today."

Adele crossed her arms, leaning against the frame. "You're certain of it?"

"As certain as I can be," he said, softly, looking up at her. "Why? Have you found something different?" His eyebrows rose. "Any thoughts on the killer?"

Adele just shook her head, sighing as she did. "Afraid not. Dead ends so far. Ms. Mayfield and Joseph Dupuy had very little in common from what I've seen. Another murder might be the only bread crumb we have left to guide us to the killer unless we find something *now*. Another death simply isn't an option!"

Leoni slowly pursed his lips. "Let's both of us hope, together, it doesn't come to that."

"Either way, today will be the next attack. If we don't find him soon, we won't be able to do anything about it. Someone's going to die."

CHAPTER FIFTEEN

Agent John Renee leaned back in the soft, frayed couch down in the basement of the DGSI. He detected the faint odor of what some might mistake for cleaning solution, but really originated from the bubbling distillery he'd set up here nearly three years ago. On the wall, two pictures were tacked to the chipped paint, displaying images of his old military buddies.

John frowned as a memory resurfaced.

A bleeding body on a bleeding table. A killer hiding in the pantry, laughing at him. A small, skeletal frame of a man. One of his eyes dead, dull, gleaming out from beneath an upturned hood.

The man had said, "Gerard; he was your copilot, wasn't he? Six of you in total, wasn't it? Does it weigh on you? You call me a monster, Agent Renee. But you've killed more people than I have. And you enjoy it, too, don't you? I can always tell. You dirty dog."

John clenched his teeth, glancing once more at the picture tacked to his wall. How had the monster known his co-pilot's name? What else did he know? The same killer who'd taken Adele's mother. The same killer who'd escaped him in Paris.

He remembered Gerard. A man of the hills, a rough man. A man after John's own heart. They'd flown more missions together than the rest of the team combined, both of them having signed up at a young age. John at sixteen, with forged papers, in between stints as a ferryman; Gerard at seventeen, the same year.

John swallowed, shaking his head softly. Gerard was the brother he'd never had. More of a father, really. Though only a single year had separated them, Gerard had been John's protector in the military. Saved his life on more than one occasion, and when all was said and done, John hadn't been able to repay the favor.

The only survivor of the helicopter crash. Sabotage, some said. Others had whispered the bird had been damaged *in base*. John had looked into the allegations, but why would someone in their own crew sabotage the helicopter? He'd decided it was just a rumor. Either way, it wouldn't bring back his brothers. Wouldn't bring back Gerard, or the rest of their tight-knit family.

He hadn't lasted long in the military following it.

John grunted and shook his head, trying to focus on the task at hand. In one hand he clutched the cool shell of a martini glass filled with moonshine. The other steadied a laptop on his long legs.

Adele might think he'd phoned it in—she might assume he wasn't interested in solving the case. But nothing could be further from the truth. The fact that Elise Romei's killer had escaped from him haunted him still. Andrew Maldonado, the sole witness to the crime scene, was still in a coma.

John needed to prove himself and yet... next to Adele, trying to solve a case with her again—it had felt different. She'd gone cold, it seemed. She hadn't laughed at his normal humor, nor had she wanted to talk to him, it seemed.

Now she was back on the train and he was back at headquarters.

He sighed, pressing even further back into the well-used couch.

"What have we here?" he murmured to himself, prying his gaze away from the photos on the wall and glancing at the progress bar on his computer screen above the compiler he'd run.

Names. Names from Italy. Names from France. Names from the train company and names from ticket booths.

Not first class this time. John was sick of the first-class passenger list. Now, he'd decided to go back, to check coach, to check layovers, to check everyone. The murders—if that's truly what they were, and he still wasn't certain—had occurred in the first-class compartments. But that didn't mean the killer was also there.

He took another chug of bitter beverage and then lowered the glass, rubbing at his eyes. He hadn't slept, instead combing through the names through the night, pulling them apart a piece at a time, narrowing down the passenger list. And checking it mostly manually.

Now, the progress bar of the final compilation, which he'd originally sorted, came to an end. Only one name. One name from coach who'd been on LuccaRail and the Normandie Express on the given dates.

One lead.

John's bleary eyes narrowed and he leaned into the white and blue light emanating from his computer. A retired train-hopper. An arrest record. Arrested for assault but the charges were lowered to disturbing the peace...

John followed the cursory information, pulling up the man's file. He paused, rereading a line, and then went still.

The man's name was Isaac Lafitte. Nothing stood out there. But one of the arresting officers in the assault had made a report… John reread the line in question and murmured, "Ah… Mr. Lafitte, what have we here?"

Isaac Lafitte's wife had died the previous year, all of a sudden. She'd been young, too—in her forties. Died from a heart attack according to the report.

John stared at the name. He pulled out his phone, frowning to himself as he dialed in the number provided for Lockport Enterprises, the overseeing company for both train lines. He waited as the phone rang.

"Thank you for calling Lockport Enterprises," came a robotic voice. "If you know the number of the extension you are dialing, please—"

"Let me speak with someone!" John growled into the phone.

The robotic voice continued, uninterrupted, listing the directory. "If you are calling the mailing office, please press one. If you are calling for—"

"Let me speak to someone!" John shouted, his voice rising.

"If you would like to speak with an agent, please stay on the line."

John felt his knuckles clenching tight around the phone, his breath coming quickly now as he resisted the urge to crush the device in his hand.

At last, the robotic voice was replaced by a very human one which said, "Hello, Colette speaking, how can I help you?"

"Agent John Renee," he said, still growling. "DGSI. I need travel itinerary for a client of yours."

"Oh, well, I have a note here to transfer you to managerial. One second."

"Don't put me on—"

Music started playing over the phone and John found himself grinding his teeth, resisting the urge to scream at the ceiling. A minute passed with John sitting on the couch, then another—which saw his martini glass emptied of all contents—then a third, which saw his martini glass arching through the air and smashing against the far wall.

"Hello?" said a voice.

"Agent John Renee," he repeated, grinding out the words through gritted teeth. "I need travel records. We already have clearance. And the number I'm using is logged as a federal line. Now give me the information I'm looking for, or I'll make sure every tax auditor I know gets your name and the name of everyone in your bloody family!" John hadn't realized he'd been shouting until the silence followed.

He exhaled slowly, and then waited.

"Ah, yes, I recently spoke with Executive Foucault. Would you mind providing your badge number for verification?"

John sighed and complied with the request.

"Excellent, thank you, Agent Renee. How can Lockport Enterprises be of service?"

"I need travel records for a previous passenger of your LuccaRail and Normandie Express."

"All right, shouldn't be too difficult. One moment."

John heard muttered instructions in the background suggesting the manager wasn't the one actually logging the information in their system.

"Name, please?"

"Isaac Lafitte," John said. "Traveling coach."

"I see in our records the last list requested was for first class, are you—"

"No, not first class. Coach. Well?"

"Ah, one moment."

More muttered words, and the sound of a clacking keyboard far removed from the phone. Then the voice on the other end said, "Isaac Lafitte, you say? Yes, I have his records right here."

"Any indication of how many times he's traveled with you?" John asked.

"I'm afraid we don't tend to keep information like that for more than a month, which is the billing cycle turnover. But… well, hang on… Interesting."

John perked up, pressing his phone even more tightly against the side of his face.

"Mr. Lafitte did travel with us, yes, but he's not done."

"What do you mean?" John asked, his frown deepening, transforming from irritation to curiosity in a moment.

"I mean," said the manager's voice, "that Mr. Lafitte bought a ticket this morning."

"This morning? Where?"

"Normandie Express again. Strange that. He got on for the French

70

leg, then got off when the rail was sequestered, but now he purchased another ticket for the trip into Germany."

"He just bought it you say?"

"Yes. He should have boarded only an hour or so ago. Also he purchased a room in one of the first-class sleeper cars. Room three, it looks like."

"Anything else?"

"Yes, perhaps it isn't important. But our two previous trips with Mr. Lafitte, he rode coach. This time, though, it seems as if he has booked first class."

"First class, you're sure?"

"Certainly."

"Is that all you can tell me?"

"I'm afraid we don't keep an extensive deposit of client information. All we have is the name and ticket information. Is there any other way I can be of—"

John hung up, jamming his phone in his pocket and rising to his feet. Adele theorized the killer would strike once per day and perhaps, once per country. Which meant it was either a strange coincidence that Mr. Lafitte was back on the train for its German leg the day following the last death.

Or John had singlehandedly found the identity of the murderer.

CHAPTER SIXTEEN

Adele far preferred Agent Leoni's first-class quarters to the solitary confinement of her hellish sleeper car room. She sat in a lavender love seat, listening as Agent Leoni listed off, in a quiet voice and with the door to his unit closed, what he'd found so far.

"Apart from the argument the first victim had," Leoni was saying, "he also had a history of flaunting his cash. At least that's what some of the other passengers said."

"And you think it got him killed?"

"His wallet was missing," said Leoni. "After he was found dead, maybe a half hour following according to the coroner, it was noted his wallet had vanished."

"A crime of opportunity?" Adele suggested, leaning on the cushy bed and feeling, for the first time, some comfort on this train.

"Or a motive," Leoni replied; he nodded seriously, glancing out toward the window framed by raised drapes as the train chugged along, having left the station and now moving toward the German border.

Adele studied Leoni's silhouette, the scrunching of his brow, the way he spoke English nearly perfectly. Firsthand experience told her he was fluent in multiple languages, knew how to fly a plane, and was as professional as they came. It also didn't hurt that he looked like he belonged on the front cover of a magazine at the grocery store.

She found her own lips curving into a smile as she watched him, the sunlight reflecting through the window, catching his face in a soft glow.

He noted her attention and looked over, smiling that crooked grin of his. Good-natured as ever, he said, "What is it?"

She shrugged but didn't look away, watching him a moment longer, realizing now that though the compartment was first class, it wasn't large enough to provide much distance between them. The door was closed, the room their own.

He continued smiling, either clueless or unperturbed by the thoughts now moving through her mind.

"Leoni," she said, carefully. "I wanted to ask you something—"

Before she could finish, her phone began to buzz and she jolted.

Adele glanced down as she fished out the device and then went stiff.

John was calling.

Strangely, her first emotion was panic. It took her a second to realize how silly this reaction was.

Adele cleared her throat awkwardly, pushing off where she sat on the edge of the first-class bed to go stand by the shut door as she answered the call. Her gaze fell on Leoni, who raised a quizzical eyebrow, but her attention was directed to her old partner.

"I have a lead," he said, gruffly. "Have a second?"

"I'm—yes, a lead?"

John paused for a moment. "Are you alone? Can you speak freely?"

"I'm—no, I'm with another agent. But yes, I can speak freely."

"Another agent? Foucault didn't mention anything about—"

"Not DGSI. It's Agent Leoni from Italy. He was the one working the other half of this case."

"Oh. Right. Christopher, yeah?"

"Mhmm. What lead?"

John took a moment, it seemed, to gather himself but then said, in a slow, careful tone, "I suppose you can share this with Lenny too, if you like."

"Leoni," she said.

"Whatever. There's a train-hopper on board with you now. He has an arrest record for assault, and his wife died last year of—get this—a heart attack. On top—he was on both the LuccaRail two days ago, and the Normandie Express yesterday."

Adele frowned, pressing her back against the door. "Hang on," she said, "he's here today? The passengers were put on other trains when we sequestered the staff."

"Right," said John, "which makes it strange, doesn't it? He bought another ticket for the same train. Looks like he moved up from coach to first class."

"Do you have a name?"

"Isaac Lafitte."

Adele pressed the phone to her shoulder, muffling the speaker, and looked at Agent Leoni. "Do you know anyone by the name of Isaac Lafitte?" she asked, hesitantly.

The handsome Italian agent thought for a moment, but gave a faint shake of his head. "Was he first class?"

Adele shook her head, phone still pressed to her shirt. "Not on the

LuccaRail. In Italy, it sounds like he was in coach, but he was also on the Normandie."

Leoni's eyebrows ratcheted up and Adele gave a significant nod. She lifted the phone now and said, "When did he board?"

"Just an hour ago," John replied. "He's in first class right now. Car two, room three."

"Excellent. Thank you, John."

"You're welcome," he said, his tone strained.

Adele hesitated, wondering if she should say anything else. Wondering if he was expecting her to. She hadn't expected John to take this case seriously, but then again, he'd been an agent long before she'd shown up. Just because she didn't approve of his methods didn't mean he wasn't effective. Still...

"I..." she began.

But she'd left it too late. John spoke over her at the same time, "See ya around." Then he hung up.

Adele sighed, holding her phone for a moment in a still hand, and then, shaking her head, she turned away and regarded Leoni. "Isaac Lafitte is in car two," she said with a significant tilt of her eyebrows.

"That's..." His frowned followed. "Hang on."

Leoni pushed off the bed quickly, wearing an immaculate Italian suit, like he was heading out to some dinner party. The suit was clearly tailored and he had twin panther-eyed silver cufflinks on either wrist. He pushed open the door and Adele quickly followed, both of them moving down the car.

Adele stopped in front of the third door, furthest from Leoni's room. Car two.

Adele shared a significant look with the Italian. "This is it," she murmured.

He nodded, raised a fist, and then knocked three times. "Hello, Mr. Lafitte!"

"DGSI!" Adele called, knocking as well, framing the door by standing opposite Leoni, her shoulder pressed to the wall in case the door was flung open.

"Quit your yelling!" came a cranky voice from within the compartment.

Adele gestured quickly at Leoni and he took a step back from the door, distancing himself in case Isaac Lafitte was armed.

"Open your door, sir!" Adele called. "We need to speak with you."

More grumbling from within and then, eventually, with an air of much reluctance, the door was pushed open, half an inch at a time, by a familiar man. The same loud-mouthed passenger who'd refused to relinquish his luggage earlier and who'd cursed out the valet. She blinked in surprise, but covered quickly. Robert had always said: trust your instincts.

The man's expression hadn't altered at all in the last hour. In fact, he seemed even more cantankerous than when they'd first interacted.

"What?" he snapped.

Adele flashed her credentials and mimed pushing the door open even more. "Mind if we chat?"

The door stayed exactly where it was, half ajar.

"Bug off," he snorted. "You got a warrant?"

"No warrant," said Adele, testily, "but we need to speak with you in regards to an ongoing—"

The door was pulled shut, cutting her off. Adele blinked and glanced at Leoni, who shrugged back at her, then looked to the door once more. "Excuse me?" she called, knocking even more loudly this time.

By now, the couple who'd bordered the train first were peeking out from the room between Leoni's and Lafitte's. They were standing in the hall, eyes wide, watching the spectacle. Adele made a faint shooing motion, and the couple ducked back into their room, but kept the door open, apparently wanting to catch all the details.

"Mr. Lafitte!" Adele called. "Open up or we'll have to get the conductor, sir!"

This time, the door slammed open and caught Adele across the shoulder, sending her reeling back into the cool glass of the near window. "Leave me the hell alone!" Mr. Lafitte shouted, shaking a fist at Adele. In one hand, it looked like he was now holding a hefty silver pitcher which he was wielding like a cudgel.

Leoni took a step toward Adele as if to see if she were all right, but Lafitte seemed to interpret this as an aggressive motion. He swung his pitcher, aiming for Leoni's skull. The Italian agent moved like water over marble. In one swift motion, he ducked under the blow, his left arm rising, catching Lafitte on the other side of his swinging arm. The first-class passenger cursed as the pitcher was sent clattering to the ground, but the sound died a second later as a swift open-handed strike to his throat sent him doubled up and gasping at the floor.

75

Adele stared, impressed—she hadn't realized Leoni could move that quickly.

Lafitte wheezed, both hands now reaching toward his neck, and he stumbled, nearly slamming his head into the open door.

"You're all right," Leoni said, in a strangely comforting sort of voice. "Take deep breaths, you're fine." He patted Lafitte on the back, but used the same motion to grip the man firmly by the collar and drag him away from the silver pitcher and the open doorway of his room.

As he pulled Lafitte away, Leoni glanced at Adele. "You all right" he asked, the concern in his voice cranking up a few notches.

Adele grunted, rubbing ruefully at her shoulder. "Fine," she muttered. Then she flanked Lafitte and with Leoni at her side, they pushed him along in search of a more private space for questioning.

CHAPTER SEVENTEEN

Something about the way they smiled brought to mind the leer of a corpse. He strolled through the first-class car, his eyes ahead, not quite glancing to the left or the right. He kept an easy, carefree grin on his lips. Kind eyes.

That's what some people said. They thought he had kind eyes.

But behind those eyes... what lurked in his thoughts... perhaps not so kind. No—not so kind at all.

He smirked to himself as if recollecting an inside joke; the authorities couldn't find him. They were back on the other train. But that was the beauty of this: he never stayed on the same train. No. That would be too easy. This new train... this one provided all sorts of opportunities. He passed an older gentleman who was chatting with one of the waitresses who shuttled food from the dining car to those too lazy to get it themselves. The kind-eyed man felt a sudden jolt of disgust. He glanced over, frowning, appraising. Was this the next one?

Could it be?

The older man looked up, caught his eye, and then smiled. A frail hand gave a soft little wave.

No. Perhaps not.

The kind-eyed man continued on his way, giving a quick dip of his head in return greeting. He neared the back of the first-class car, near a felt-covered card table where a small group of players were shuffling a deck and preparing for another round of Texas hold'em.

He stepped forward, curious. The kind-eyed man always did enjoy poker, in all its variations. His life reminded him of a poker face. He knew how to bluff, deflect, how to hide what he was holding most of all. Certainly, hiding in plain sight was an acquired and crucial skill given his pastime. He'd finally summoned the nerve to start... Years of hoping, dreaming, of watching degrading images and videos on his computer late at night. But the thoughts were no longer enough; the pictures and movies—poorly acted—didn't satisfy. Even some of the actual videos he'd found, of the *real* thing...

Revenge in its purest form... But it didn't provide the same...

satisfaction. The same fulfillment. Nor was it a true vengeance against the guilty parties.

No, now that he'd summoned up the nerve, this—he realized—was far, far better. Anyone who'd ever said revenge wasn't satisfying had never experienced it or were simply lying through their teeth. It satisfied more than sex, more than drugs, more than power. It satisfied in a deeper way than any might imagine. So deep, it almost felt like it welled from his soul.

A woman caught him watching and for a moment, she got a glimpse of his eyes. He cursed, glancing sharply away, trying to shove his thoughts down, to focus on smiling, nodding. But the woman stared at him, then sniffed, raising an eyebrow and turning to mutter darkly to a friend next to her.

The kind-eyed man heard the words "leering… creep…"

He frowned, fixing his gaze on her for a moment. She glanced up and scowled even deeper and turned promptly to mutter to her friend some more.

The kind-eyed man smiled widely now. He'd found his next message. Those pretty lips, painted with lipstick more expensive than some people's rent, those manicured fingers which likely hadn't done a real day's work in their life—eventually, soon, they would be before him on a seat of judgment. And he'd already decided the verdict.

Guilty as sin.

The judgment would have to wait. Not yet—preparations were in order. But soon—tonight, perhaps? Yes, very soon.

CHAPTER EIGHTEEN

Adele, Leoni, and Isaac Lafitte had sequestered in the staff break room in the dormitory car for the train employees. The break room had been cleared, and the large television was now off, its blank, black face staring down at the table where Adele, Leoni, and Isaac sat.

Isaac wasn't in cuffs just yet, and he was still ruefully massaging at his throat where Leoni had jammed his thumbs.

"Do you know why you're here?" said Adele.

"Bitch, do I look like a clairvoyant?"

Leoni frowned. "Careful with your words."

But Adele held up a hand. "No, it's fine," she said. "Let him *express* himself. Just know, Mr. Lafitte, right now, all that's standing between you and a prison cell back in Paris is me. I'm here to determine if you're a person of interest."

"A prison cell?" he spat. "Don't be ridiculous. I didn't do anything." The man's face was now beet-red, and he had a thin unintentionally monk-like circle of hair due to male-pattern baldness. His nose was bulging, his chin jutting in defiance. Everything about the hue of his skin suggested it had been well treated with more than one drink from the dining car.

Adele held up a finger. "For one, you slammed a door into me."

"Didn't know you were cops," he replied.

"I announced myself when I came."

"You said Deegee sigh. What's that supposed to mean?" He seemed ready to add another expletive at the end, but Leoni raised an eyebrow and the man left the sentence as it was.

"DGSI," Adele said. "Federal investigations."

"Pshaw. I don't know anything about that. Why should I? Do I look like a government employee to you? Crooks, the lot of you."

Adele massaged the bridge of her nose. Why couldn't these interviews ever be easy? "Look," she said, "Mr. Lafitte, I'm investigating two murders."

"Likely murders," Leoni inserted.

"Right. Likely murders. And *you*..." she emphasized the word, "are

79

the one common point between the two."

He snorted. "Impossible. Get better at your job."

"I'd really like to. Do you think you could help me with that?" Adele said, proud that she'd managed to keep most of the exasperation from her tone. "Were you on the LuccaRail two days ago?"

"Course," he spat again. Then he dipped his head and massaged his temples, shaking his head. "Not good to be cooped up like this," he said, tugging at his collar again and glancing around. "Not good at all."

Leoni frowned at Adele but she pressed. "Sir, LuccaRail, were you on it two days ago?"

"Yeah, so what? I was on it two weeks before that as well, and two weeks prior to that in addition. What of it?"

Adele blinked. "Hold on, you were on the LuccaRail three times in the last month?"

"Six," he retorted. "I ride the train. Often."

"How often?"

"Every day sometimes. Depends." He pulled at his collar again, his face reddening further, and he shook his head, causing his sweaty hair to shift and sway. "It's too hot in here," he murmured. "Can we open a window?"

To her surprise, Leoni hopped to his feet, moved over to the nearest window, and cracked it a bit. Lafitte didn't provide much in the way of a thank-you, but at least he didn't curse them out again. He inclined his face toward the open window, breathing softly as if taking in the breeze.

"Sir, are you all right?" Adele asked, slowly.

The man glanced back at her and swallowed. He returned to looking out the window at the passing countryside as the train finally moved from France into Germany. As he watched the rolling hills and the green flatland, his eyes seemed almost to mist over and his breathing came more regularly.

He sighed, staring through the window, watching the passing countryside. "I didn't kill anyone," he said.

"Mind if we check your luggage?" she said. "We can get a warrant."

It felt like a shot in the dark, given his previous reactions to them, but now as he stared out the window, he almost seemed mesmerized, as if entranced by the passing terrain.

He grunted and shrugged.

"Is that a yes?" Adele pushed.

Isaac Lafitte continued to stare out the window, watching the tranquil greens and blues.

"I'll take that as a yes," Leoni murmured.

Adele nodded and got to her feet, turning toward the door, but Isaac grunted, still staring out the window. "Not you—the one who opened the window. I have nothing to hide."

Adele slowly lowered back into her seat. Leoni gave her significant look, raising an eyebrow in greeting to his single curl of hair.

"I'm fine," she answered the unspoken question. "Go on—I can handle this."

Leoni shrugged, but then left, making sure to leave the door propped open as he moved back toward the first-class sleeper car to search Lafitte's belongings.

"So you ride trains often?" Adele asked, hoping to keep Lafitte in this new, calm, lulled state.

He continued to ignore her, staring out the window. Then, as if the question had only just reached his ears, he murmured a soft reply. "Often as I can. Daily. It helps."

"Helps?"

"Yes," he said, turning to her now. As he looked away from the window, his eyebrows lowered again, as if he were somehow stepping into a frigid room without a sweater. He clenched his teeth. "Helps. Damn you all. Can't a grieving man be left in peace?"

"Grieving? Why are you grieving, sir?" Adele pressed. "Your wife?"

He stared at her. "You know about Claudia?"

"I was told. She passed away last year, didn't she? A heart attack?" As she said this last part, she watched his reaction closely.

But there was nothing except a flash of grief across his countenance and a muttered prayer beneath his breath and he returned to staring out the window.

A few moments passed, with Adele unsure what else to say. It made sense he'd be grieving his recently deceased wife, if he wasn't behind her death. Heart attacks weren't exactly uncommon—perhaps it was a coincidence... But why would someone ride a train so often?

It helps... he'd said. Helps with what?

Adele heard a soft clearing of a throat and she glanced back to find Agent Leoni had returned, carrying a brown bag with him.

Isaac Lafitte turned, and his face reddened. "What are you doing with that?"

"You said we could search," Adele reminded him.

He hesitated, his eyes flickering as if in recollection. "Did I really?"

Leoni nodded sympathetically, but held up the bag toward Adele. "This was the only item in his cargo hold. No toxins—no poisons. A small bottle of pills, though." He held up an orange container with a white lid and gave it a little shake.

Lafitte noted this and it seemed as if he were now being confronted by an old enemy. "Pshaw," he spat. "Throw those away for all I care. They make me dull—muted."

"What are they?" Adele asked.

Leoni answered first though, "Mood stabilizer," he replied, softly. "My mother used to take the same sort—though a lesser dosage."

"Joy-stealers," Lafitte added, shaking his head. "I'm supposed to take them twice a day. Bah! Riding the train is better. It keeps me sane. Those devil things," he said, pointing at the pills, "make me forget. Forget *her*..." He trailed off and looked out the window again. In a murmur he added, "I wouldn't have them if my daughter hadn't made me promise."

Adele looked from Lafitte, feeling a flash of sympathy herself, and regarded Leoni. "Nothing else?"

Leoni shook his head, gently placing the satchel next to Lafitte. "I confirmed with my own people as well." He nodded toward the man staring out the window. "He's been riding trains daily for nearly a year now. Almost every day."

Lafitte glanced at them after a moment, his eyes widening in surprise as if he hadn't realized anyone else was in the room with him. "What?" he snapped, as if someone had interrupted him on a phone call. "What do you want? Who are you?"

Adele sighed, exhaling a long breath. She stared at the man; did she really think a man of this mental capacity could kill without detection? The murders were planned, careful, speaking of a shrewd, *sharp* mind. There was nothing sharp about Mr. Lafitte.

At last, massaging her temples, she said, "Mr. Lafitte, we may have more questions for you in the future, but you're free to go. Mr. Lafitte? Hello?"

But he seemed lost in his own thoughts, his eyes transfixed by the blurring countryside. Adele hesitantly rose to her feet, with Leoni standing next to her. For a moment, they both glanced uncertainly toward the seated train-hopper. But he had his luggage clutched close to his chest, his chin now pressed against the soft leather on top.

"I…" Adele trailed off. She shook her head. "Have a good day, Mr. Lafitte."

She turned, following Leoni from the compartment.

CHAPTER NINETEEN

Margaret Moulin arose and moved from the first-class compartment to stretch her legs. She smiled at Bella, her traveling friend and companion and confidant. The young woman gave a little wave back, smiling as she did, then turned to her boyfriend, who sat in the lounge chair of the first-class compartment next to her. Margaret could almost sense their topic of conversation shifting as she moved from earshot. She knew they would be discussing her, because Margaret herself had few other preferable topics of conversation besides the lives of those proximate, but not too close.

She hesitated as she moved into the adjacent rail car. This one was empty, with most of the seats removed and signs on the walls advising the car was temporarily out of use for remodeling. Something about the empty space fascinated her. She wondered what sorts of stories would accrue over the years, the decades, delicious secrets and salacious rumors uttered in every corner eventually.

She smiled to herself at the thought. Only an hour or so ago, she'd been talking with Bella about the strange man who'd wandered through the first-class compartment and stared at her. What an odd duck. Probably smelly, too. He'd had the look of a nasty sort. It wasn't easy to tell, but in the eyes... or the clothing, and especially the shoes.

Margaret felt certain the character of a person could be immediately discerned by the state of their wardrobe. The older the clothes, the more shabby the shoes, the less reputable the person.

She'd stake her reputation on her little scale of gradation.

Still, there had been something in that man's eyes... the way he'd watched her. It hadn't felt lecherous—a look she'd become accustomed to while traveling for business among dirty people. Rather, there had been a hunger there of a different variety...

And a rage...

She shivered at the recollection, suddenly feeling very alone in the empty train car poised for remodeling.

She picked up her pace, moving across the space toward the opposite exit which led to the dining car. A drink. She needed a drink—

not that she imbibed as much as Bella did. The poor thing, drinking at all hours of the day. How her boyfriend, Richard, put up with it, heavens knew. Then again, Richard himself was not unfamiliar with a beverage or two. And if her sources were to be trusted, he'd started seeing another girl on the sly.

She smiled to herself, grateful she wasn't as caught in her vices as Richard or Bella. Really, it was magnanimous of her to befriend them.

As she neared the divider between this car and the next, leading to the dining space, she pulled up.

A dark, lumpy jacket had been left, draped just in the shadows of the doorway.

She looked over her shoulder, her spine suddenly prickling. For a moment, it felt as if she were being watched. She shivered, but the compartment behind her was empty.

For the faintest moment, she thought she glimpsed a silhouette flash across the glass divider door leading back to the first-class compartment.

She froze, her heart in her throat. But no one came through the door. She relaxed, breathing a bit easier now, and turned.

A man stood in front of her.

Not just a jacket, but a person, she realized. He'd been hiding in the shadows.

Her eyes widened and for a moment she caught a scream. "What are—" she began.

Then her eyes widened further as she recognized the man in the jacket. The same man with the raging eyes who'd been ogling her back in the first-class compartment. He'd been waiting for her.

"I—I don't—" Her voice began to rise, but before she could scream, his face stretched into a smile and he lurched toward her, one hand clamping over her mouth.

She felt ill all of a sudden, her stomach twisting in stark terror. She could only hope he didn't defile her. What would the others say then? She remembered after the little incident where one of their mutual friends was assaulted behind a bar, it had been the talk for months...

"Help!" she screamed. Except the hand covered her lips, and her voice came out more like a strangled gasp into his thick palm.

He was strong, and though she tried to fight, she couldn't move. Her eyes strained in their sockets, desperate, gaping. A flash of a needle near her check. A needle? She realized then, the man was holding a syringe.

It plunged toward her neck once—he cursed as if he'd missed his target. Another sharp jab, and then... a hot, sluicing sensation spreading through her veins.

It hurt, like a bee sting. She staggered and kicked out this time, hard, catching him in the shin. The man grunted and his grip loosened for a moment. She reeled back, screaming now at the top of her lungs. The man's eyes flashed and for a moment he just stood, seemingly unfazed by her yells. But also, his eyes hungry again, as if he wanted to drink in the sight...

Her knees felt wobbly all of a sudden. Her head spun.

Margaret reached up, her hand at her chest; the warm feeling from her neck had now spread down her shoulders, her arms, her legs, her heart.

It felt like something was squeezing her insides, twisting. Then the pain—unimaginable pain.

The man grinned now, watching, then he looked up, as if noting movement beyond, and quickly turned, scampering back toward the dining car, away.

Margaret could barely see. She dropped to the ground, gasping. Something was squeezing her chest. The man in the jacket slipped through the doorway, stepping through the shadows.

She tried to scream again, but her lips were completely numb.

Now she heard the patter of feet. A sudden cry of voices. Was one of those Bella's? Dear God, she hoped Richard wasn't there too. She couldn't imagine the embarrassment of explaining this. They'd talk about it for weeks...

They'd...

The shadows moved in above her. She heard voices echoing as if from down a deep well, but she couldn't react, couldn't move, couldn't speak.

Darkness came complete.

CHAPTER TWENTY

The train stopped in Karlsruhe in Germany, just north of the Black Forest, on the other side of the French border. Adele and Agent Leoni moved toward the open doors in the dining car which exited onto a small metal embarking platform, and down some stairs to the train station.

"Your partner will be here, you say?" Leoni asked, regarding Adele.

She nodded distractedly, scanning the platform ahead of them. "Yes—he won't be joining us on the train, just meeting at the station to go over case notes. Rest stop is for a couple of hours," she said, but then glanced back to the Italian. "I don't know if it matters, though."

"Oh?" His eyebrows went up.

She paused in the threshold of the train, one foot on the first step and the other still in the compartment. Most of the train's residents interested in moving through the station to stretch their legs or grab some food had long since left. A few still remained on the train, either sleeping, or in the case of Mr. Lafitte, his eyes fixed through the window, as if seeing something no one else could.

Adele frowned, shaking her head at the recollection of the interview. Mr. Lafitte had initially struck her as loud, abrasive, and potentially dangerous. Now, though, after double-checking his claims with the travel company, it became clear that traveling by train was a near daily experience for the retired train-hopper.

It all just felt so sad now. She sighed and shook her head again, regarding Leoni. "No. The killer didn't stay on the same train last time, and I imagine he wouldn't this time either."

"He?" asked Leoni. "You're assuming a male? Poison is often a woman's weapon, no?"

Adele shrugged. "Perhaps—I'm not ruling anything out. My point is that we might be wasting our time here..." She shook her head and stepped off the train onto the platform. Leoni followed behind, and as he did, he reached out suddenly, steadying himself against her and murmuring, "Sorry!"

She looked back at him and his face had gone red in embarrassment as he stared accusingly at the bottom step of the metal ladder. "Blasted thing tried to trip me," he muttered.

Adele watched Leoni, and the way he shook his head, flustered. His right hand, though, still pressed to her shoulder—warm, comforting, and strong all at once. Adele didn't say anything, but allowed him to lift his hand in his own time. As he did, though, she felt a strange flicker of regret.

She opened her mouth, uncertain what she would say, though wanting to say *something*. But just then, her phone began to ring.

Adele cursed, held up a finger, and turned her back to Leoni, answering.

"What?" she said, a bit more crossly than perhaps she ought to have.

"Happy to hear from you too," retorted the voice of John Renee.

"What is it, John? We're here. You still coming to meet up?"

"I'm on my way now. Crossing the border."

"All right, we can wait. I was just telling Leoni we need to tackle this case from a different angle. I don't think the killer is on board."

"Right—*we*. Whatever. Look, Sharp, I can pretty much verify that second part. Killer definitely isn't on board."

Adele went still, staring out across the station along a row of coffee shops and small cafes in the side of the passenger areas. Through the glass walls of the station, she glimpsed the distant greens of trees and slopes in the Black Forest.

"You sound certain," she murmured, biting a lip. "Did he attack again?"

"Yeah. Germany this time. The Green Coach."

Adele felt her stomach clamp and her breath come in a gusting rush. Another death. *Dammit,* she thought. But now wasn't the time to freeze. She cleared her throat. "Also with Lockport Enterprises?"

"No. Different owner, different country this time too. But new victim—a young woman, late twenties. Also had a heart attack, this time witnessed by at least six others."

Adele found her hand tightening around the phone and she resisted the urge to scream.

"Adele, what is it?" Leoni asked from behind, as if he could sense her consternation.

She glanced half back. "Third victim," she said, biting off the words. Then she said into the speaker of the phone, "You still coming?"

"Yeah, I'm hurrying. Just one thing—the train in question can't be sequestered now. It's currently moving through the Black Forest mountains, in the wilderness. No train station for at least another hour or two, and no access roads for emergency vehicles either..."

Adele, though, didn't share the frustration seeping from her old partner's tone. She shook her head quickly, and said, just as fast, "No, that's good news, John. Excellent, in fact."

A pause on the phone. Static, and for a moment she thought she'd lost him. But then, a second later, John said, "Good news? How?"

"If the train is still moving," Adele returned, her grim smile widening, "then that means the killer is still on board."

"I mean... you're not wrong. But for that to matter, we'd have to reach the train first—before emergency vehicles show up, or before they reach a station. I don't think German authorities will go for holding back a train full of their citizens for our sake."

"We don't have to worry about that headache," Adele insisted. "As long as we can keep that train moving, then the killer has to stay put. We just need to reach it first."

"Hang on," John said suddenly. "I have an idea. I know how to get to the train before it stops."

"What are—"

Unable to hide the undercurrent of excitement now creeping into his voice, John said, "Just sit tight. I'm on my way."

CHAPTER TWENTY ONE

Adele stood outside the station, near a parking lot the authorities had cleared a half hour before. Now, a large ring of red traffic cones cordoned off an area the size of a tennis court. Adele stood next to Leoni, her arms crossed in the chill, misty air coming in from the mountains.

She strode back and forth, one arm bent at an angle, still crossed, but also holding her phone pressed to her ear, seemingly a permanent fixture, glued there by intent alone.

"Yes sir," she was saying. "I understand. We'll tread lightly."

Executive Foucault was on the other line, his rasping voice continuing, "I'm serious, Adele. No unnecessary risks. We finally have the Germans playing ball. They won't stop the train until they feel they have to. But we're in a tight window here—very tight."

"I understand. But sir, I—"

Before she continued, though, she felt a hand tug at her wrist. She glanced over, half-expecting John. But the Frenchman was running late, and she hadn't been able to contact him since the last call. Instead, it was Agent Leoni, who was holding out his own phone and staring at it, his eyes wide.

In a whisper, he said, "Coroner got back."

"Executive," Adele said, quickly, "I'm sorry, no, I'm really sorry, just one second." She pressed the phone to her shoulder, muffling it, and looked at Agent Leoni, waiting.

Faintly, Adele could hear a voice calling from the speaker, "Agent Sharp! Hello! Can you hear me!"

She winced but waited for Leoni, and he spoke quickly, as if not wanting to intrude, but there was an urgency to his tone. "Look," he said, holding up his phone.

Adele stared, and saw a clear image of what looked like someone's neck.

"What am I looking at?"

"Right there, see it?" He pointed, and she leaned in.

"Here's another picture—he circled it!" Agent Leoni flicked the phone's image, and it moved to the same picture, but this time, a small, black circle had been drawn on it.

The circle was around a tiny red area that looked no more significant than a pimple.

"What am I looking at?"

"The coroner thinks that's an injection site," said Agent Leoni. "Says they think this was where a toxin might have been administered."

Adele kept her own phone pressed to her shirt, staring, wide-eyed. "Are you serious?" she said.

"As the grave," Leoni returned.

"Do we have results from the tox report?"

"Not yet, but there's a rush on it now. We should get those by the end of the day."

Adele nodded urgently, then raised her own phone again, and said, "Sir, the Italians just got back; the coroner thinks it's a definite murder. Found an injection site. Toxicology report is running late, but it should be here soon."

"So, you want to keep the train on the move?" Foucault asked. "The Germans are getting restless, and I have to give them an answer now."

"Yes, yes sir, please, keep the train moving. This just confirms that it's a serial killer. But, sir, while we can't stop the train, could you ask them to slow it down a bit? That might help us to catch up with it, and to give us more time before the passengers get to the station."

"All right, I'm trusting you on this, Adele. Like I said, tread carefully."

"You have my word."

The Executive said something else, but Adele couldn't hear it on account of the sudden whirring sound above.

She looked up and then, at the top of her voice, called, "Sorry, sir, I have to call you later." She hung up, gaping as a black and green helicopter moved over the train station, headed toward the circle of traffic cones. She stepped back to an even safer distance next to Agent Leoni as the helicopter descended, the blades spinning and whirring, and then coming to touchdown on the asphalt, with a deafening sound of chugging blades.

She stared up toward the cockpit and spotted two men. In the passenger seat, with a grin on his face at the look of Adele's surprise, John was giving a small, sarcastic wave.

"Is that our ride?" Leoni asked.

"I guess so," Adele muttered. "Be careful and try not to throw up. John sometimes enjoys bumpy rides just for the sake of annoying his passengers."

Leoni gave a chuckle which was nearly lost in the swell of the wind, but the smile faded as he stared at her. "Are you being serious?"

In answer, Adele sighed, then picked up her pace, approaching the helicopter. A third victim, a train on the move, a clock running out of time. They had to reach that train. And if the helicopter was the way to do it, she couldn't say no.

She reached the metal bird and pulled herself up by a steel rung into the back seat. Leoni followed after, and to her satisfaction, she noted John's grin fade a little as he got a look at the Italian.

Adele donned the headset John extended to her, and then into the microphone, shouted, "You got us a pilot?"

"Pilot came with the chopper!" John shouted back, patting a hand on the shoulder of the man at the controls.

Adele just shook her head in disbelief. John was resourceful if anything. "The Executive is having the train slowed down. German authorities are cooperating for now. But we're on a clock!"

The crackle of the speakers over her headset said, "Right—this is an old flying buddy of mine. Call him Casper. He's a friendly ghost, and he's gonna be the one bringing us in."

Adele glanced at the second man in the cockpit at the controls, but he was still staring out the windshield, as if equal parts bored and at ease. Judging by one of the tattoos on his right arms, he was ex-military.

"Casper just has a helicopter lying around?"

John frowned now. "Casper owes me *three* favors. You better believe he dropped everything to pay off at least one. Forget about that shit though, we need to get moving."

"How are we going to get onto the train?" Adele shouted, leaning forward a bit in the cushioned chair, though that did nothing to increase the volume of her mic.

John turned in his seat, his own headset pressing against his headrest, and said, with a devilish smile, "We're going to have to rappel down onto the moving train." He gave a wink in Agent Leoni's direction. "Hello there, my spaghetti-eating friend," he called. "Hope you're in the mood for a little bit of a fly."

In answer, Leoni shut the helicopter door and stared straight ahead.

John chuckled, patted the pilot on the arm, and they began to lift, carried up by the chugging helicopter blades, in search of a moving train, and, in Adele's opinion, an incredibly reckless attempt at boarding it.

Then again, if it meant they could catch the killer, it just might be worth it.

CHAPTER TWENTY TWO

The afternoon settled in hazy sunlight as the chopper blades cut through the sky, spinning the air in flurries around them. John's pilot friend dipped low, scraping the hazier wisps of mist rising from the Black Forest. In the distance, Adele spotted the train, pulling along at a hampered pace per Foucault's instructions. Still, her chest heaved as she stared, her eyes locked on the small trail of movement meandering through green slopes and over wooden bridges.

"This is insane," she muttered into her microphone, her hands clasped in her lap.

John heard her over the headset, and he nodded in the front seat. She could just see the corner of his lip twisted in a smirk. "That's one word for it," he said, his eyes fixed through the windshield. He gave some indeterminable motion with his hand which seemed to prompt a response from the pilot. The helicopter dipped lower, scything above the trees and coming nearer and nearer to the train below.

They were gaining. The train was moving at a snail's pace—at least there was that mercy. Adele wasn't interested in some action move scene, ending in a horrific helicopter crash, screaming agents, and a fiery blossom in the frame.

Slow and easy. Then again, nothing with John seemed to be easy. This whole thing was his blasted idea anyway.

As if reading her thoughts, John looked back, his dark eyes peering at her in the back of the helicopter. "You're the one who said we had to catch the train before a station. Well… here it is. No roads lead to this part of the forest."

Adele shook her head, the headset shifting as she stared out the window, toward the quickly approaching locomotive. "Now what?" she said.

John winked at her, and for a moment, it almost seemed like things were back to normal between them. Nothing like a little bit of high octane adrenaline to set priorities straight. As John moved, he reached out and *accidentally* pushed his hand roughly against Leoni's chest. The Italian grunted, but then John moved between the front and back

94

seats, sliding his lanky form in the spacious back compartment between Leoni and Adele.

Then he pointed to three harnesses hooked on the back of the helicopter. His headset was now dangling over the front seat where he left it, so he mimed placing the harnesses over their heads. Adele reached out, snaring one of the grained fabric vests and passing it to Leoni. She passed another to John, then, still muttering darkly to herself, she removed her headset, placed her own harness over her head, pulling her arms through the gaps in the crisscrossing straps and tightening the metal buckles across the front.

"All right?" she shouted, moving her lips emphatically to help the two men read what she was saying despite the noise. "Now?"

John pointed toward a metal loop attached to twin pulleys as thick as hubcaps by the sliding door of the helicopter. He then leaned across Adele, brushing against her, and snared a thick loop of black rope which lay on the ground, already attached by a metal hook to the safety hitch.

Then like a rock-climbing instructor, John first looped the rope through his metal clasps on the front of his harness and then mimed to Adele, pointing at the simple clasp and showing her how to release her own.

He pointed at his chest, held up a finger, then pointed at her and Leoni and mimed glasses.

"Watch and learn? I get it," she shouted back.

John was no longer grinning, though. He turned back toward the sliding door beneath the safety hitch. He had a strange light in his eyes which Adele had witnessed on more than one occasion. When things got heavy, bullets started flying, or the agents attempted some sort of life or death stunt, John always seemed in a sort of heightened state, his eyes wide, his nostrils flaring. A light didn't spark behind his eyes so much as it died. As if he were switching off any sort of fear, empathy, desire. John was terrifying in that way if you were on the wrong side of the law. But if you were wearing the same uniform? Adele couldn't think of any place safer.

She knew John had a history with helicopters. He'd flown them before—once on the ski slopes in the Alps. But prior to that as well, while still serving his country overseas. She knew it had ended in tragedy. But it was just like John to refuse to allow past pain to claim prizes for current endeavors.

She glanced at Leoni, who was still shifting uncomfortably.

By now, John was signaling instructions to the pilot. The helicopter dipped, just a bit, and now Adele could see through the glass in the side door, the train below them. They began to slow as well, and the helicopter adjusted. Adele could almost hear the scrape of the chugging wheels beneath them now, over the sound of helicopter blades.

She looked to Leoni, whose face had paled. He didn't seem perturbed by the harness—and she reminded herself that Leoni had a pilot's license of his own. Still, he looked worried. When he caught her watching, though, he flashed a quick thumbs-up, then pointed toward John, if only, perhaps, to redirect her attention.

She felt a flicker of concern. Normally, Leoni was always calm, collected.

"This is insane," Adele muttered to herself.

John made a spinning motion with his finger, the pilot pulled on the controls, and now the rotating blades above made a different sort of noise. Were they slowing? Falling?

No... Adele realized. They were trying to fly directly over the train, so they could rappel down.

"Insane," she muttered again. "Batshit."

And then John flung open the side door. Wind blasted into the cabin, sweeping across John and ruffling his slicked back hair, sending it flying. Adele's own eyes strained at the gusting wind. They were slowing, though, likely to match pace with the train.

Adele's heart jumped in her throat as she watched John, rope looped through his harness, reattached to the second pulley on the hitch. Then he looked at her, flashed a thumbs-up, and jumped off the side of the helicopter. Adele leaned forward, one hand out, bracing where she still sat strapped in her seat. She unstrapped, gripping a metal handle near the open door, and leaned forward, watching as John shimmied down the rope.

The pilot seemed to be keeping them on a steady course, at least for now, guiding them along just above the train. She could see three compartments ahead of them. Thankfully, the train was going so slowly, it allowed the pilot to keep up with relative ease.

John moved down the rope, expertly managing his pulley the way he'd indicated to Adele, using the clasp release to slow or speed his descent. For a moment, Adele wished she'd had a bit more time to acclimate. It seemed simple enough though.

At last, still leaning and watching, she stared as John landed on the ceiling of one of the train compartments. He released his clasp at last, letting the black rope slide free, and it shot up all of a sudden, pulled in by a whirring motor on the pulley.

Adele glanced to the pilot, who was still staring, fixed at the train in front, using it as a guiding post to keep them steady.

She glanced at Leoni, then down at John. She swallowed, then looped the rope through her own harness how she'd seen John do.

Batshit. All of it. But no time to hesitate. The whole point of this was to catch the killer before he had a chance to flee, to hide amidst a station of passengers, or slip off the train when it got near a crowd. No—now wasn't the time for fear.

She swallowed once, pulled a couple of times on her clasp, testing it, and then she turned back toward the open air, eyes fixed on the interior of the helicopter cabin. Leoni was watching her, still a bit pale, his eyes wide.

She flashed a thumbs-up, then jumped.

The pulley did its work. As she began to fall, her body weight counteracted the motor in the pulley and she descended, rapidly, but not too quickly. Still, she squeezed her clasp, slowing the descent. The wind seemed to carry her, knocking her about as she fell from the helicopter above, aiming for the slowly moving train below. She glanced between her feet where John was crouched low, one hand out, braced against the metal ceiling, one hand upraised, gesturing at her as if guiding in a landing plane.

She continued to descend, heart in her throat. For a moment, she noted a turn up ahead. The train began to maneuver, changing its course. Adele cursed as her feet suddenly swayed over the open terrain, passing across wilderness and the untended wild of the Black Forest. Suddenly, it didn't seem like they were moving so slowly after all.

Then, as she locked the clasp on her vest, keeping the rope from spilling through, and herself dangling in the air, the wind buffeting around her, the pilot above seemed to course correct. There was a sudden uncomfortable jolt in her harness as the helicopter readjusted on the train's new course.

Then, still swaying more comfortably than she would like, she released the clasp and descended the rest of the way.

Her feet thumped into the metal ceiling of the compartment, and she felt John's firm hand reach out, gripping her arm and steadying her where she rocked and swayed on the moving locomotive.

She managed to duck, crouching low and reestablishing her center of gravity. Then, breathing heavily, her hands pressed to the cold metal roof, she released the clasp and the rope slipped out like spaghetti sucked through pursed lips.

A few moments passed and she gathered herself, realizing now she was kneeling on the top of a train in motion. John knelt next to her, one hand braced against the roof for three points of stability.

He grinned at her and said, over the sound of the train below and the helicopter above, "You okay?"

"Yeah, think so," she shouted back.

"See, it wasn't that bad," he began to say. But then, a second later, he looked up and his eyes went wide. The blood seemed to suddenly drain from his face.

Adele turned too, frowning, and she spotted Leoni descending. But he was moving far, far too quickly. She could hear him cursing in Italian as he plummeted, heading straight toward them at a breakneck pace.

CHAPTER TWENTY THREE

"John!" Adele cried, reflexively. There wasn't enough time for any more words.

Agent Renee cursed and staggered to his feet, holding out a hand as if to try to catch and break Leoni's fall, reacting, it seemed, on instinct alone. Leoni, though, seemed to jolt and jar for a moment, his hand feverishly working at the climbing vest's clasp. There was a whistling sound of the rope going suddenly taut, and Leoni's body bounced, jarring painfully.

Now, though, he hung suspended nearly twenty feet above, not moving at all. Below, John began to shout an instruction. But the train began to move again, turning down a mountain pass and now heading directly toward a tunnel in the side of the slope.

"John!" Adele shouted, pointing.

Agent Renee gritted his teeth and gestured at Leoni. "Release the second clasp!" he shouted. "It's caught—the rope's caught!"

But his words were lost in the wild sounds and panic of the moment.

Leoni descended another few feet, then got stuck completely. The helicopter above maintained course, but Adele realized it wouldn't be able to for much longer, without slamming into the cliff face.

"Christopher!" she shouted, one hand still braced against the roof of the locomotive, her eyes wide and peering up toward the Italian. "Drop! You have to drop!"

He was nearly fifteen feet above the top of the car now, but still too high. It wouldn't be safe. There was no other option, though.

"Christopher!" she screamed.

Agent Renee and Adele watched helplessly, braced against the metal roof of the train. The tunnel beyond was quickly approaching, despite the calm pace of the engine.

Adele heard another curse as the Italian agent marked his trajectory. Then she glimpsed a flash of silver as his hand procured something sharp from within a pocket. Teeth gritted, he began sawing feverishly at the rope.

The helicopter pilot above began to move, having left it until the last second. Now, he had to rise above the mountain slope or slam into it. There was no more time.

Leoni's body, still dangling from the rappel line began to sway as the helicopter did. With one last cry of extraordinary effort, Agent Leoni managed to saw through the rappelling line, in a puff of small black fabrics. Then, with a shout, he tumbled, falling from the sky and rushing toward the train, completely unsupported now.

The helicopter veered away at last, completely, but it had altered trajectory in those last moments, causing Leoni to gain momentum and swing forward as he fell.

Agent Leoni was not just sent plummeting, but tumbling toward the edge of the train. Adele lurched forward, trying to snag her new partner. But she missed, and Leoni struck the top of the train. Then he began to roll, sliding along the slick metal surface.

John, though, moved fast. He was taller, lengthier than Adele. With a herculean groan, his fingers managed to snag the Italian agent's shirt, gripping him tight. Adele heard a loud cry of pain as John's arm extended. Leoni's fingers scrambled against the slick surface as he yelled, trying to find purchase, but it was too late. Above, Adele glimpsed the helicopter just barely move in time to avoid the mountain at the same time as Leoni's momentum from his fall took him tumbling over the edge of the train.

"No!" Adele screamed.

But it was too late. She watched in horror as the Italian agent fell. John, though, growled, his hand whipping over the edge of the train with Leoni, his arm extended, braced, his whole body beginning to slide. With a shout of relief, Adele realized he'd managed to keep his grip on Leoni's shirt, despite the plummet.

Desperately, she scrambled to the edge of the metal roof and reached over, noting the handsome agent kicking his feet and trying to latch onto the slick ceiling with both his hands. She reached down and gripped at Leoni's collar where John also had him.

"On the count of three!" she said.

They were nearly at the tunnel.

John shouted, "Three!"

And together, they both hoisted Leoni up and onto the roof again.

The Italian agent yelled as he was pulled alongside them. They

100

whistled into the tunnel, and all of them went flat, low, with the flashing lights from inside the train reflected in the dark cavern.

Adele lay motionless, her cheek pressed against the cold metal, gasping, staring sightless in the black. She could hear the others next to her, also breathing heavily, cursing and muttering to themselves. She heard Agent Leoni in the dark offer up a small prayer of gratitude but then groan in pain. He might have managed to maintain his balance on the train, but he'd fallen fifteen feet. She wasn't sure how he'd landed, but by the sound of things, it hadn't been comfortable.

They all stayed low, hunkered down as the train moved through the tunnel and then burst out the other side.

And like that, they were amidst the trees and sunlit forests, and Adele could breathe a bit easier. She sat up slowly, feeling the wind brush across them, and pointed toward the hatch in the top of one of the cars.

John and Leoni both nodded. The Italian agent was still wincing, and John was massaging the crook of his elbow. Together, the three of them moved along toward the hatch, which John opened.

First Leoni, then John, and Adele, at last, dropped down into the compartment through the hatch.

Her feet on solid ground once more, the sound of the wind suddenly shut out by the insulation of the cabin walls, Adele could hear her own breathing, coming heavy. The other two gasped raggedly, and Leoni winced, stepping delicately on his ankle. John continued to massage his arm, shaking his head and muttering, "That was fun, wasn't it?"

They stood in the compartment that looked to be mid-remodel. There was no furniture and the walls themselves were bare as if they were simply in a moving steel box. Adele stared towards a lump in the middle of the room, beneath a white sheet.

"John," she said, hesitantly.

Renee glanced over, frowning, then spotted the source of her attention. He muttered to himself but moved forward, and with his foot nudged the edge of the fabric. A cold hand jutted out from beneath the sheet.

"I think that's our body," Adele said, shivering. Normally, corpses were removed before she reached the scene, or if they were still there, the coroner would be as well. But in this case, with a moving crime scene, the police hadn't managed to reach the train yet. No access roads. Hence the stunt with the helicopter. Which meant that no one

101

had touched the body—at least not yet. No one except the killer.

Adele glanced around the bare compartment, toward the glow of light coming through the reflective glass divider at the back. Through it, she could see faces peering into the car where they had landed.

She glanced at the Italian agent and muttered, "Are you okay?"

Leoni winced and tested his leg, pressing it against the ground and hissing through his lips. "I'll be fine," he muttered. "Thanks," he added, glancing at John.

"Whatever," Renee muttered. "You're fine—I got your back, just try not to screw anything else up." Then he turned promptly away from the Italian and began to march across the compartment toward the glass divider with the faces peering into the car.

"This should be interesting," Leoni muttered to Adele, his eyes tracking the lanky Frenchman.

Adele sighed and shrugged, but then winced sympathetically. "Are you sure you're okay?"

Leoni hesitated. "I should be fine."

"Need a hand? You could balance on my shoulder."

John looked back from where he'd paused in front of the divider, frowning. Agent Leoni noticed this and just said, "No, I should be fine, thank you."

Adele nodded, watching as the Italian began to limp along after John toward the divider between the cars. She regarded the lump beneath the thin sheet for a moment, frowning in thought. And then, with a sigh, she followed after the two men. The killer was still stuck on the train with them. One of the faces staring out at them, perhaps? Someone hiding? The train was about an hour away from the nearest station. An hour to solve this. An hour before the German authorities got involved. An hour before the passengers were allowed to disperse, or escape.

***

The man with kind eyes peered over the shoulders of the other gawkers at the three new arrivals on the train. He'd heard the helicopter, glimpsed it through the window. Now, he spotted three new passengers, all of them with the physiques and intense scowls that might accompany law enforcement.

Had they really rappelled in?

He cursed to himself. He'd intended to disembark at the next station, making good his getaway in the crowd. Already, he'd planned out three routes of exit in case the authorities tried to sequester the train. But now, on the move in the wilderness? A much harder feat.

The kind-eyed man listened to the murmurs and mutterings of the passengers around him. He tried to look sufficiently surprised himself.

"Who do you think they are?" one was saying.

"I think I heard a plane earlier," another replied.

"No, they're maintenance. They came from the service hatch. Probably just here to take care of the body," another said.

"That woman," a third added. "I think I recognize her from the papers. Isn't she the one who landed that plane on the autobahn?"

A chorus of conversation followed this final comment, accompanied by the murmurings like a bunch of clucking hens.

The kind-eyed man resisted the urge to grab one of the chickens and wring their necks right there. No, he needed to keep a low profile, to blend in. Three wolves had wandered into the chicken coop, but he was in sheep's clothing—he'd avoided capture so far. He refused to feel afraid. Not for these new arrivals—feds by the look of them. Not for the passengers around him. Not for anyone. Fear was for the uninitiated.

He glanced through the window at the passing terrain—the train had slowed now. Could he possibly leap from the locomotive? Get a running start?

No. Not yet. Too conspicuous. It would be like sending a flare declaring his guilt. Besides, it wasn't like they *knew*. How could they? He'd been careful—covered his tracks. Moved from train line to line, country to country. Careful, planned, inconspicuous.

No, they were simply ruffling feathers. Trying to spook him to scamper. But he knew better. He wouldn't bite.

And so he stood shoulder to shoulder with the sheep in the first class, watching through the divider into the second compartment as the three new arrivals moved toward the door.

He could just faintly hear the helicopter now in the distance, disappearing. For a moment, one of the figures stopped in the compartment. An attractive woman, with shoulder-length blonde hair and a runner's physique. Her eyes... though. Something about her eyes reminded him of himself. A fire there. A vengeance.

Those eyes settled on him for a moment, staring at him through the

103

window of the divider, it seemed. And then she looked away, gesturing at the two men to follow as they approached the first-class car, leaving the body beneath the tarp on the cold floor behind them.

CHAPTER TWENTY FOUR

"Calm down," Adele said, trying to keep her tone soothing, rather than exasperated. The first-class compartment was packed, it seemed, with nearly fifteen passengers staring over Adele's shoulder, toward where Renee and Leoni were examining the corpse. The train itself was high-end, but nothing like the Normandie Express. Instead of old-fashioned seats and wooden trim, this train was sleek and metal with comfortable, modern seating and flashing reading lights above personal television screens.

Adele stood in the doorway, trying to shoo the civilians back into their car. "Nothing to see," she insisted. "Please, this is an ongoing investigation."

"And who are you?" someone demanded.

Adele sighed, flashing her credentials and then stowing her wallet. "DGSI," she said. "I'm working with Interpol and with the cooperation of the BKA. Everything is going to be fine."

"Told you they weren't bloody maintenance," someone muttered.

"How should I know? They came through the ceiling," another retorted.

Adele massaged the bridge of her nose but then looked up again, alert, glancing around. No time for tiredness. No time for an adrenaline crash. Someone on this train was a serial killer. Someone here? Watching her?

Her eyes landed on a woman in an expensive sweater with a scarf made of what looked like mink. She had perfectly manicured nails and a nose seemingly—and likely—sculpted by surgeons. The woman stared at Adele, whispering to a handsome man next to her beneath her breath. Another man, thickset with a quivering jaw, was talking loudly, trying to be heard over the others. "Why is BKA involved?" he was saying. "She had a heart attack, didn't she? That's what you said, Dr. Lawrence." He glanced toward another woman, who was leaning against one of the cool windows displaying the slowly moving terrain.

The woman shook her head quickly and said, "It has the markers of it. But that's a cursory observation. I'm a general practitioner besides, it isn't like—"

"Well?" said the young woman with the mink scarf. "Why *are* you here?"

Adele tried to keep track of all of it, but the flood of discussion was beginning to give her a headache. She gritted her teeth and said, "Please, back to your seats, or recreations. No one should be within ten feet of this door, understand?"

Everyone stared blankly at her, eyes blinking like a bunch of owls. "I said get back!" Adele snapped.

Reluctantly some of the passengers complied, but the rest of them continued to gawk. Adele glanced helplessly over her shoulder. John, noting her expression, stepped away from the body, his glare out in full force. The tall, scar-faced agent stepped into the first-class compartment and in a booming voice he said, "Get the hell back before I make you, dammit! We might be on German soil, but unless you want a French ass kicking start moving!"

Half the passengers, at least, likely didn't understand the Frenchman's tirade in his native tongue, but his tone communicated more than enough, and the rest of the passengers quickly scarpered, following Adele's directive and leaving their gawking posts by the glass divider.

Adele sighed and gave a nod of gratitude toward John, before turning and rejoining him in the bare, mid-remodel train car.

She shut the divider behind her, sliding it.

For now, at least, it didn't seem as if so many eyes were fixed on her or the corpse. Leoni was still wincing where he stood on his injured ankle. John was glowering at everything unfortunate enough to acquire his gaze and Adele passed a hand through her hair, stepping off to the side so the passengers couldn't view her from within the other compartment.

"Well?" she said, her voice low, quiet in the still car. "What now?"

John shrugged at her, still scowling. "I got us on the train. You're the one who had the great idea to get us here before the station. It's your show, Adele."

Leoni didn't comment, but he looked at her as well, an expectant quality to his gaze. She frowned, nodding to herself. For a moment, as she stood over the body draped in the thin white fabric, she felt a familiar chill. The same sense she'd had back in Foucault's office when he'd first introduced the case…

106

Something was off... something horrible.

But why was she feeling it now? She shook her head and glanced from John to Leoni, trying to catch her bearings. She said, "All right, I think we split up. We have about an hour before the train reaches the nearest station. Then, no telling what German authorities will do. I don't think most governments are in the habit of sequestering a hundred citizens in order to catch a *possible* killer. We need to get this done before the culprit has a chance to slip away, or get his alibi straight."

"What do you propose?" Leoni said, wincing as he did and favoring his right ankle.

Adele nodded determinedly, shoving aside the sense of foreboding rising in her gut. "We search the train front to back. We question everyone. Hard. John, you start with the sleeper cars, Leoni, you go to the last compartment."

"Hang on," John interjected. "I want the back."

Adele frowned. "What does it matter?"

John shrugged. "I don't need a reason. Limpy here can have the sleeper cars."

Adele resisted the urge to roll her eyes. "All right, Leoni, you can take the sleeper cars, John, you get the back. Sound good?"

"Great. And where are you going? Let me guess, with Casanova here."

Adele glared at John for a moment, but he shrugged off the comment with a snort and glanced toward the body again. Adele said, "I'll be interviewing first class and see, once they've calmed down a bit, if they've seen anything untoward."

"Big word that," John said. "Untoward. Think our Italian friend needs some help with the French?"

Leoni replied in flawless French, "I understand. Let's stop dawdling. We're running out of time."

Adele gave a quick nod of agreement and then turned, splitting off toward first class and allowing John and Leoni to head toward the back compartment of the train in the direction of the sleeper cars and the caboose.

***

Adele sat across from the beautiful young woman in the mink scarf and her arm-candy boyfriend. Both of them kept shooting glances at

107

each other as if sharing an inside joke as Adele settled before them, across the table divider. Every so often the woman's eyebrows would twitch and the man would snort as if she'd told a funny joke. Occasionally, she caught them glancing at her shoes, or at the somewhat wrinkled sleeves of her suit.

Adele frowned after this second eyebrow tilt, followed by not-so-hushed giggling.

"All right," she said, injecting a bit of Renee into her voice. That quieted them both and they stared like deer in headlights. "Tell me again, what happened?"

"Oh, it was horrible," the woman in the scarf said; she'd given her name as Bella. "Well," she said, drawling, "Richard and I were quite close to Margaret. Though she was a frightful gossip, mind you."

Richard, the handsome hunk, nodded along, smiling benignly.

"I'm really quite upset by the whole ordeal—a death on the train. And you're here," Bella continued. "Which means..." she raised her eyebrows and leaned in a bit, her mink scarf shifting. "Murder?"

"I can't comment on an ongoing investigation," said Adele, testily. She leaned back in the stitched leather padding of the rear-facing seat. A slow blur of greens and browns passed by outside her window as the train continued to trundle along, heading in the direction of the nearest station where the authorities would be waiting.

"Well... Margaret was our friend. So if anything *did* happen to here, I feel like I have a right to know!"

"I can't comment on an ongoing investigation."

"Oh, bother," snapped Bella. "What good are you, then?" She slumped back, crossing her arms and jutting her lips in a pout. Seeing this, Richard leaned in and kissed her cheek, whispering in her ear, and Bella glanced toward Adele's ears and gave a quick smirk.

"All right," Adele said, clearing her throat. "Maybe I wasn't clear. I'm not here to talk to you. I need you to talk to me. What happened last you saw Margaret?"

Bella, though, pretended like she hadn't heard, staring petulantly out the window. Richard, the quieter of the two, but seeming the more intelligent—or at least, more aware of impending danger—saw the lowering of Adele's brow and the forming of her fist and quickly said, "Not much, she just left to go powder her nose, if you know what I mean."

Bella, as if unable to avoid this line of speech, added, "We think she

108

was going to get a drink. She was a frightful drinker, wasn't she, Richard?"

"Quite so."

"So she went to get a drink, or to the bathroom?"

"She went through there," Richard said, waving a hand airily toward the compartment where the body still lay. "We heard a shout and got up to go check."

"Poor Margaret," Bella said slowly. "Imagine how her parents will react when they hear the news. Killed on a train—so young. Probably drunk, I'd guess. And I'm usually right about those sorts of things, aren't I, Richard?"

"Yes, dear, yes, very."

"The doctor on board didn't mention any scent of alcohol," Adele continued. "Did you see anything else? Anything that might matter?"

Margaret and Richard shared a look, glanced back at her, and both shrugged. They began to nuzzle again, with Adele still across from them, and Adele resisted the urge to grab a nearby cup of ice from one of the server's trolleys and toss it in their direction. Instead, she reached out, snagged a water bottle, and tipped it back.

"Umm, sorry," said a hesitant voice. "Excuse me, but those are for passengers only."

A young valet was frowning at her, wearing a red staff uniform and shaking his head. An older man was watching the entire exchange from a window seat across the aisle, seemingly trying to hide a smirk.

"Sorry," Adele muttered, placing the bottle back on the cart. "Did either of you see anything… *useful*," she added, emphasizing the word.

The old man was still smiling, and the young valet frowned at the sullied water bottle, now placed among the other, unopened ones. Delicately, as if lifting a soiled napkin, he reached out with two fingers, plucked the bottle, and handed it back to her. "I suppose it's all right just this once," he muttered. "Just don't tell my boss—he'll have my job." This last part was muttered beneath the young valet's breath.

"Oh—he's a hard boss, is he?"

"He's fine," said the valet quickly, glancing sharply over his shoulder. Then the young man leaned in, whispering. "The woman you're talking about, I saw her. She left the car, that way—" He pointed in the direction of the glass divider separating first class from the remodeled car with the body. "Towards the restrooms. Then I heard something break."

"No, no," the old man interrupted, shaking his head. "It was a scream. And I heard it too."

"You both heard a scream?"

The valet hesitated, glanced at the old man, then shrugged. "I heard something. Those of us in earshot went to investigate, and found Margaret—that's her name, right? We found her on the ground…"

The old man was no longer smiling and he shook his head, staring out the window now. "A true pity, that," he murmured. "She was so young, so full of life."

The valet, who couldn't have been much older than twenty, nodded as well, shooting a look toward where Bella was now making out with Richard. His cheeks reddened and he hastened quickly away, leaving Adele and her purloined water bottle sitting across the table from the two lovebirds.

As best as she could muster, Adele concealed her look of disgust, rose to her feet, and moved back through the compartment in the direction of the restrooms. She passed the body, pausing for a moment, alone in the still car and staring down at the unfortunate soul now turned a pile of cold sinew and flesh. She sighed, standing beneath the hatch they'd used to enter the train.

"Sorry," she murmured, quietly, staring at the body of Margaret. "I'll find him. I promise."

Then she turned, heading in the direction the valet had mentioned— the restrooms. She pushed through the door to the women's, on the far side of the second car, just within the divider. She scanned about, but the restroom was clean and smelled faintly of cinnamon apple candles, which were tastefully arranged around the sink.

She glanced behind the toilet bowl, in the sink, along the walls. No blood splatter—nothing illicit. No clue.

Adele frowned, crossing her arms as she stood alone in the bathroom, its slight shaking responding to the motion of the train on the tracks.

No one saw anything—one of them heard a loud crash, another heard a shout. No physical evidence on the body she'd been able to see. And the sense of foreboding was now claustrophobic, practically smothering her like a blanket made of wet wool.

She was missing something… she had to be.

But what?

CHAPTER TWENTY FIVE

John massaged the bridge of his nose, regretting his decision to switch with Limpy the Italian. The back of the train was where the staff hung out on break, and while John was glad he'd never learned German, he was beginning to wish he'd never picked up English either.

A couple of the older staff—from the dining car judging by their uniforms and spaghetti sauce splatter, were giving him a piece of their mind. They were both equally wrinkled, short, and had introduced themselves as Mr. and Mrs. Something. Smole? Smile? No.

John shook his head. It was so hard to concentrate with such incessant yammer.

Mr. Something was shaking a finger in front of his bald head. Mrs. Something looked nearly identical to her husband, even with nearly matching spaghetti stains, with the addition of a wig that resembled a dry mop in John's opinion.

"But Agent," Mr. Something was moaning, "if there is a body on the train *why* won't we stop? Surely it's not sanitary…"

John winced, straining to pick up the English words amidst the German accent. He shook his head slowly, still massaging his nose. "We are heading to the nearest station. There, people may disembark. Now, about the dead woman. You're saying you never saw—"

"We told you already!" said Mrs. Something, shaking her head and causing one of her chins to jiggle. She reclined in a lazy boy, staring up at a screen displaying some sort of dance competition. She took a long sip from a lager and glanced up to where John stood in the center of the compartment, trying to maintain the attention of the couple. "No clue who she is. Dinner hasn't even been served. We're not on shift till then anyhow."

"You mentioned," John said, grimly. "Do either of you know *anything* useful?"

The husband and wife shared a look, and the woman brushed her mop-like locks out of her eyes, and then she shrugged. "Not sanitary to be with a body," she said. "How's that for useful?"

John clenched his teeth now. For one, he'd managed to get nowhere

111

interviewing the staff. For another, he wasn't entirely certain what the word "sanitary" meant in English. He'd have to look it up. But either way, he was sick of the complaining and needed some air.

"Say," called another voice from the back of the compartment.

John looked and watched as two new waiters entered and collapsed on a soft couch. "Are you with the feds?" one called. "We hear there's a body in the new compartment. Is it true?"

John turned his attention to this new, younger couple, desperate and hoping perhaps they'd have something useful to add. "Do either of you know the victim?"

"Victim, see," said Mrs. Something. "There's a killer on the train. What did I tell you?"

Her husband nodded darkly and leaned in a bit closer to his wife, where he sat on the arm of the chair.

The young couple looked nervous now. "There's a killer here?" one of them said.

"Forget it," John replied, turning.

"Wait, hang on," said Mrs. Something. "I'm not done speaking with you!"

"I've got to go!" John cried over his shoulder, muttering darkly and stomping out of the staff's compartment. He moved on into the mostly empty dining car, hearing the swish of the door behind him, grateful to have escaped the incessant nagging.

John waited a moment, exhaling softly through his nose, then looked up. Besides a bartender preparing for the evening rush, there was only one other person in the room.

Agent Leoni was wiping sweat from his forehead and thanking the bartender as he reached out, gingerly accepting a small bag filled with ice.

For a moment, John stared at the Italian. He didn't like the man. He wasn't sure why yet, but John didn't like him, and his instincts were rarely wrong. Well… then again, he hadn't liked Adele when he'd first met her. But she'd been teachable. His own personality had managed to rub off on her a bit, making her at least tolerable company. This Leoni fellow though—shifty, unreliable. He could see it in the eyes.

What sort of idiot sprained their ankle while doing a simple rappel down from a helicopter?

John snorted to himself as he reluctantly moved across the compartment toward where Leoni sat, more to escape the staff behind him than for any desire to become proximate with the Italian.

Leoni took the small bag and lifted his foot, pressing the ice to his ankle just beneath the pant leg. Were those pants from a dinner suit? They seemed far too fine for work clothing. Again, John resisted the urge to scoff—though not too hard. The Italian clearly wasn't a man built for action.

His mood souring even more as he approached Leoni, John came to a halt. "Anything?" he said, followed by a grunt.

Leoni dabbed at his ankle with the ice for a moment, as if finding a tolerable position, and then he pressed it against his leg, emitting a soft sigh of relief. He looked up, regarding John. "Nothing," he said. "Sleeper cars were mostly empty—and those that weren't had little to tell me. I understand the victim wasn't very well-liked by everyone, though."

"Who is," John riposted. He sighed, passing a hand through his hair. "Shit, it just feels like we're wasting time."

"Mhmm. The train will stop at the next station; to not do so would be negligence. How do you think Adele is faring?"

"Adele?" John asked, regarding the Italian again. The smaller man had symmetrical features and a messy strand of hair threatening to get in his eyes. Not the ideal haircut for a shooter, John thought to himself. Even the smallest distractions could prove costly. "Let's reconvene with Agent Sharp then. Need a hand?"

Leoni looked at John, then shook his head. "I'm fine," he said, pausing for a moment to gather his strength. "Thanks, though," he added as an afterthought. "For... well, for saving me back there."

John just grunted. "Stop falling off trains and you won't need saving."

"I can't argue with that." Leoni, gritting his teeth, the ice pack tucked in his sock, lowered his leg and began limping back toward the front of the train. He paused for a moment in the doorway. "You and Adele aren't much alike," he said.

John glowered. "Maybe you just don't know her as well as you think."

"Perhaps. She's a good agent—you're fortunate to be partnered with her." Then he turned, limping back up the train.

John followed, frowning as they went.

***

113

The kind-eyed man gnawed at a fingernail, staring absentmindedly out the window to the first-class car, doing his best not to look like he was eavesdropping. Every so often, he would glance over to where the blonde agent was talking to other passengers.

She was getting close. Too close.

She looked up and he glanced sharply away again, watching the passing countryside. There was something off about that woman—something too keen, like an overexcited hound on a hunt.

He needed to get away from her and from her giant companion and his limping sidekick. But how? The train was still on the move, still amidst the trees. The nearest station was a half hour away. A half hour...

He glanced back again and now found the woman was watching him.

A half hour was too long. She was getting too close. He flashed a smile, hoping to disarm. A second later, he realized his mistake—she wasn't watching him, she was staring out the window.

He cursed to himself and began to move away, pushing further toward the front of the train. As he did, he felt some relief, abandoning the blonde agent and her soul-searching gaze. She was onto him.

He could feel it. What if she *hadn't* been looking out the window? Maybe she had been watching him.

They were so close. Why would they have rappelled onto a moving train unless they knew who he was? They were playing with him! Toying with him!

He felt a flash of anger surge through his chest.

They were no different than the others. Not at all. Something about that woman's demeanor spooked him. And if they were just like the others... maybe they also needed to be reminded of the way of things.

He nodded to himself, glancing down and noting his hand was shaking as he moved along the final compartment leading to the engine.

If she really was getting that close... there was always a solution.

He could kill her before she figured him out. And the next location of import was quickly approaching. The next station, in fact—a special one. For a moment, he paused, closing his eyes and inhaling deeply. He could feel the fabric of his late father's shirt, soft against his shoulders. He reached out a hand, rubbing at the smooth cloth, trailing his fingers across the sleeve.

114

The shirt even still smelled of aftershave.

A ghost of a smile crossed his lips, and his kind eyes welled up for a moment. He didn't wipe away the tears, though. His father deserved more than that. Deserved a life he'd never been given.

The upcoming station—another one of the many stops his father had frequented as a conductor. The kind-eyed man smiled, his eyes misting even more as he remembered the trips, remembered the many stops along the way. He also remembered the railroad switches.

The exchanges along the way. Each station where he'd claimed a corpse, each place had the option for a switch. And each time the railroad chose it.

But it never had chosen it for his father.

His father had traveled the same route, again and again until the stress of eighty-hour work weeks had killed him young. The train and its occupants had been allowed to switch tracks, but the conductor? Stuck. The same path, over and over and over.

The man narrowed his kind eyes, feeling a welling of sheer hatred.

He turned back, glancing in the direction of the first-class car he'd abandoned. Money had forced his father to work to the bone. Money had forced his father to strive through all hours. Money and its friends had left a young boy without his only friend at too tender an age.

And so he offered the friends of money back to the endless path. Again and again and again. First in Italy, at the initial rail switch, then in France at the subsequent one. Now, three rail switches in Germany— the first already complete.

The second rapidly approaching. The second kill would be in Germany too. Wherever the switches were.

The blonde agent was just like the rest of them. Hunting him down the same way they'd run his father ragged. Yes—yes, she needed to go.

He nodded to himself, then began to make his way toward where he'd stowed his bag. The toxin was there, hidden in an old thermos. He'd need that for what he was about to do.

CHAPTER TWENTY SIX

"Nothing?" Adele asked where she stood against the farthest wall from the body in the mid-remodel car.

John and Leoni both emitted similar sighs. "Nothing," John said.

Leoni shook his head, doing a better job at concealing his disgust—as the Italian had always been the more understated of the two—but still hinting at his frustration in the tightening of his brow, and the firm press of his lips.

"Only twenty minutes left," Adele said, looking away from the body beneath the tarp and staring out one of the windows next to a sign that read, *"Under construction."*

The passing trees and mountain passes were flattening out now, and the train seemed to be descending, looping down the slope and heading toward flatter ground. Off in the distance, on the horizon, she could see the outline of structures and buildings, and the reflection of sunlight off glass windows.

"What do we do?" John said. "We're nowhere. The killer could be anyone."

Adele crossed her arms, holding her elbows and grinding her teeth as she thought desperately, looking for some way out. She turned, regarding Agent Leoni, but he just watched her back, quiet, speculative.

"Questioning doesn't seem to be working," Adele said. "No one saw anything of use. One of the valets suggested he heard something break before the woman screamed. But just as quickly, he was corrected by an older gentleman, who said he'd simply heard a scream."

"Something break?" John frowned. "Break in what way?"

As if on cue, all three of the agents began glancing around the compartment, their eyes sweeping over the bare walls and the empty floors.

"The windows are all intact," said Leoni.

Adele took a few steps toward the first-class compartment, her eyes fixed on the glass divider. At least this time no one was staring in. But they were stuck. She'd never been at such a loss. Equally frustrating was the knowledge the culprit was somewhere on the train with them. For all she knew, he was watching them, tracking their movements as they went around like chickens with their heads cut off, from person to person, train car to train car, with nothing to show for their efforts or energy.

Something about this kindled a rising sense of frustration that blossomed into pure anger. She hated the idea of a serial killer watching, laughing, behind placid features. Had she already spoken to the bastard? Had he been in the first-class car? Maybe he was laughing at them now, giggling to himself at the thought of getting away with three murders under the noses of the authorities.

"We can't give up yet," Adele said, growling in frustration. "Twenty minutes until we reach the station. That's still twenty minutes. We have to—"

Before she could finish, she heard a soft rapping on the glass.

For one strange moment, she glanced toward the external windows, looking out at the countryside. But then Agent Leoni nudged her, and she looked toward the glass partition of the first-class compartment.

She frowned as she recognized the valet who had wanted to refuse her water. He was looking nervously over his shoulder, as if checking with the old man in the compartment for permission.

Adele remembered his testimony about something breaking. A clue? Whatever the case, it wasn't like they were getting anywhere fast.

She gestured urgently at the young man, who pushed through the glass partition and came to stand in front of John. He cleared his throat, glancing nervously around, refusing to look toward the body. His cheeks had a whitish tinge, as if he were equal parts sick and scared at the same time. John had that effect on people, and corpses just a bit less.

"I'm sorry for interrupting," he said, stammering, "I know, I know you said not to, but, just the…" He trailed off and glanced toward John, who was glaring at him.

"What?" Adele said, trying to keep her tone gentle.

The young man, who couldn't have been much older than twenty, muttered, "The conductor would like to speak with you. If it's not too much to ask. I know you're busy, and I can tell him, if you'd like, that maybe—"

"The conductor?" Adele said, slowly.

For a moment, she hesitated. She didn't have the time to be yanked

117

around every which way. But as she continued to think about it, she remembered the staff list. They had cross-referenced the same staff list, which had said two people were common between the murders on the train cars in France and Italy. The bartender, whom they had cleared. But the conductor also.

She felt a sudden shiver.

"The conductor," she said, hesitantly. "It isn't Peter Granet, is it?

The young man wrinkled his nose and shrugged. "Honestly, they switch so much, I don't know. Should I tell him you're coming?"

"Better yet," Adele said, with a significant glance toward John and then Leoni, "lead the way."

The young man turned, as if glad to be looking any direction than in John's glowering face, and then hurried off, his red uniform stiff and starched like cardboard. He walked quickly, not even glancing back, and Adele hurried along, listening as Leoni breathed, not cursing as he hobbled after them. He'd refused any help, yet she still felt sympathy for the agent. His sock, from what she'd seen, was wet, with some droplets from melted ice now seeping to the floor around him.

They had bigger concerns, though, than water damage on a few floorboards.

The young valet passed the old man who was sitting by the window. The man in question looked up, and he wasn't smiling now, a newspaper laid in front of him.

As he spotted the agents with the valet, he frowned for a moment, but just as quickly, his expression flickered, and he adopted the same smile, his eyes shining as he regarded them.

Adele hesitated, looking at the old man, but then she followed after the valet, who was quickly losing them as he pushed through the partition at the end of the first-class car, which led further into the train and up toward the engine.

The engine itself was more spacious than Adele would've thought. As they were pushed through a metal door, which was locked from the inside and required a quick knock and an announcing of their presence before it would open, Adele could feel her apprehension rising. She felt a flicker of excitement, which just as quickly gave way to nerves. She wasn't sure what lay beyond. Twenty minutes left, twenty minutes until they reached the station. Twenty minutes and the killer would get away. But the conductor had called. The same conductor had been on the Italian train and the French one. Peter Granet. Was it the same man here

118

on this third train? If so, certainly it wouldn't be a coincidence. It couldn't be. Three bodies, three countries.

It was with a rising apprehension, like a child on Christmas morning unwrapping a glistening present, that Adele stepped into the engine.

Two men in white uniforms standing by the metal door turned to resume their seats, facing a small window no bigger than a porthole. One of them picked up a book he'd left on a coffee table, and the other crossed his arms, watching them enter. Adele's attention, though, was drawn toward a man sitting next to an array of controls. The conductor wasn't wearing a hat, like she'd imagined in her mind's eye, but he stood, straight-backed, with perfect posture.

"Peter," Adele said, preemptively.

But the man didn't turn.

She pressed into the room further, staring at the back of the man's dark head. Was it the same conductor? He had the same build. Why had he summoned her?

John stood in the frame of the door, as if blocking anyone from running, and Leoni limped after Adele, moving deeper into the engine. The valet, glad to be rid of them, his work done, turned and scampered off.

Adele stared at the back of the conductor. "Excuse me," she said, "sir?"

At this, the conductor seem to snap out of his reverie from where he was staring through the elevated windshield at the front of the train. Now Adele had an even better look at the approaching city beyond. The settlement outside the Black Forest wasn't as large as Paris, nor did it seem as populated. The train station, though, would be a hub of transit. Adele knew if the train stopped, the killer would have every chance to slip away.

"Ah, yes, the federals?" said the conductor, turning fully now.

Adele felt a sudden flutter of disappointment. It wasn't Peter Granet—he didn't match Granet's picture at all. This was a different conductor than the last two. Another dead end.

"Agent Sharp," said Adele, nodding in greeting, her lips firm. "This is Agent Renee and Agent Leoni," she said, nodding to each of her partners in turn. "We were told you sent for us. We're in the middle of an investigation, so I hope you don't mind if we make this quick."

The conductor still stood, straight-backed, perfect postured.

119

Something about his stance reminded Adele of her own father. She instantly guessed he was either military or ex-police. Regardless, unlike her father, he was perfectly clean-shaven, his hair trimmed back, neat. He wasn't handsome, nor were his features striking. But there was a clean, almost maintained quality about his features. His face wasn't as weathered as someone might've expected from a man who had the same color of gray hair. His teeth, when she glimpsed them, were white, but not unnaturally so, suggesting he took care of himself.

The straight-postured conductor glanced around at the agents and cleared his throat. "I'm happy to make this brief," he said. "I've been in contact with the German authorities, and will be pulling the train into the station as planned."

Adele frowned. "Is there any way we could go slower?"

"I'm afraid that's impossible. Already passengers are complaining. In Germany, German citizens have rights." He raised an eyebrow, seemingly plucked and trimmed. "I'm sure you know this."

"I'm not asking for you to break any laws," she said, trying to hide her frustration. "But I'm looking for some help here, just a few more minutes."

The conductor shook his head. He didn't wince, he didn't apologize, and his tone was matter-of-fact and straight to the point. Though he was a conductor on a train, he carried himself like a captain in the army.

"We've done what we could. We're traveling at a third our normal pace, and we've given you ample time. We even agreed to allow you to enter through the hatch above the remodeled car. But we have a body on board. Which brings into question all sorts of hygiene issues. And on top of that, I have to get on another train within the next half hour. I'm running late as it is."

Adele sighed and glanced back toward the two men in the white uniforms by the window. One seemed engrossed in his book while the other was still watching them curiously, from beneath hooded eyes. Security? She wasn't sure.

"All right, so you have to get on another train. But we're trying to catch a serial killer, you're aware of this, yes?"

"As I said, I've been in contact with the German authorities. They've apprised me of the situation. I wish we could be of more help. As I said, we did slow the train. Are you saying you're no closer to finding the murderer?"

120

"We're doing the best we can," Leoni interjected.

Adele frowned, annoyed. The conductor obviously wasn't willing to budge. He had the air of a man who'd already made up his mind. "Look," she said, firmly, "is there anything you can do? Stall? Lock the doors? Slow even further?"

"I said I can't slow, and I have another train waiting for me."

"Come on, man," she said, firmly. "This psycho has already murdered three people. Do you really want that on your conscience?"

His eyes narrowed, and his jaw went rigid. He stared at her, and with granite in his voice, the conductor said, "My conscience is clear. I have a job to do; a job that shuttles hundreds of people around from country to country. Some of them doctors, others businesspeople, others family members. Without transportation, people like you," he said, nodding toward her, "couldn't do your jobs either. You're not the only person with a job to do on this train. And you're certainly not the most important person on this train," he said, firmly. "We're doing what we can. If you have an issue with my conscience, maybe it's your own you should examine. You had more than an hour to find a killer. And by the sounds of things, you're no closer than when you started."

"Hold on," said John, glaring from where he stood in the doorway, "if you're moving to another train, who's going to be conducting this one?"

Adele hesitated. In her frustration, she hadn't realized the obvious question. She felt a flash of gratitude at John's words. They both regarded the conductor.

"My second," he said, as if the answer were obvious.

"Hang on," said Adele. "No one said anything about a second."

The conductor shrugged. "I don't know who you've been talking to. But all trains have a second. They take over for the conductor when he needs rest, or sometimes will take over when he has to switch trains. As in this case."

"There was no mention of a second on the staff manifests."

"Sometimes they're not listed. Especially if they're not going to be needed. Think of it more like a backup plan. My second's been riding around on trains for three days without having to do anything."

"You sound reproachful," John said.

The straight-postured man grumbled and shook his head. "Gets paid nearly as much as me to do what? Sleep around in the dormitory car? Please. Regardless, the German authorities want to catch the killer as well. They'll be waiting for you at the station. That's the best we can do. That's all I have. And as you said, you've got little more than a quarter hour left."

"The second," Adele said, quietly, "you say he's been riding around for three days?"

"Not on this train. He only just boarded earlier this morning. But he's been on other trains for the last three days, without actually having to put in any work."

"He's been on *other* trains in the last three days? You know which ones?"

The conductor hesitated, pausing for a moment, then he nibbled on the bottom of his lip. "I don't know all of them. But I think one was the LuccaRail, you know it?"

Agent Leoni perked up at this answer. "This second of yours, is it possible he was on the Normandie Express as well?"

At the earnest tone in the Italian's voice, the conductor looked over, frowning deeply. "I don't know. Like I said, I don't keep track of all his trains. All I can tell you is he hasn't had to put in a day's work for the last three days—lucky him."

"And where is he now?" Adele said, her voice insistent. She felt a prickle along her spine. A second? Someone who didn't appear on the staff list. She'd cross-referenced staff from both trains. Only two hits. But if the name hadn't shown up, if he had been on the LuccaRail, the train from Italy where the first victim had been killed, then possibly he'd been on the Normandie as well. Maybe this was their connection point.

Through the windshield, she glimpsed the quickly approaching city in the distance. Soon, they'd arrive at the station. Soon, she knew, the killer would have a chance to get away. But maybe they'd been gifted a lead just in time.

"Where is he?" Adele demanded.

She stared, hard-eyed, at the conductor. She felt her stomach twist, though, as he gave an indifferent shrug. "I wish I could tell you. But I don't keep track,"

"Dormitory car," said the white-uniformed man who was reading a book.

Adele glanced over. The man was still engrossed in his novel, and he didn't look up.

"Excuse me?" Adele asked.

122

A bit of irritation crept into the reader's voice. "Johnson is in the dormitory car and has been there for the last ten hours since he transferred from the Normandie Express."

Adele felt her stomach twist. "Hang on, the Normandie? So he was on the French train?"

But the man reading his book seemed to have decided he'd already said enough. He flipped the page and ignored the agent staring at him. Adele felt a rising sense of frustration, but she didn't have time to make an issue of it. "Where's the dormitory car?"

The conductor blinked and said, hesitantly, "Next to the sleeper car. Dormitory cars are where the staff hangs out between shifts. But I have to advise you that I don't think it's possible Johnson had the nerve to commit—"

"Thank you for your time," Adele interrupted.

Fifteen minutes until they reached the station.

John was already on the move. "I know the dormitory car. I was just there," he growled as he brushed past Adele, gesturing for her to follow.

Leoni limped after them, not complaining, but moving slowly on his injured ankle and struggling to keep up.

Adele broke into stride next to John and they hastened back in the direction they'd come.

"LuccaRail, Normandie, and now here," John said with a mutter. "Think it's a coincidence?"

Adele set her jaw and shrugged one shoulder as she marched hurriedly forward. "Mighty big coincidence if so," she said. "A second. He didn't even show up on the manifests. It might be our guy, John."

"He's our killer," John said, nodding firmly. "I'd bet everything. We just have to find him before the train stops."

CHAPTER TWENTY SEVEN

"Hang on," came Agent Leoni's gasping voice as they crossed the remodeled car with the body. Adele whirled around, her heart hammering from where she'd been half jogging next to John in her effort to reach the dormitory car and the reserve conductor.

Now, she stopped next to the tall Frenchman and regarded the Italian agent where he gasped at the floor and leaned against the wall, his face very pale all of a sudden, a thin film of sweat slicking his brow.

"What is it?" Adele said, concern stretching her words.

"My ankle," he murmured, gritting his teeth. "I think it might be broken."

John grunted. "Sprained more like. Putting weight on it isn't going to help in either case."

Adele cursed and glanced around the compartment helplessly, searching for...for what, exactly? A first aid kit? A doctor? A miracle in a bottle? Leoni was injured. He'd be of no further use like this, and as much as she hated thinking it, right now, he was just slowing them down.

"Do you think you can stay here?" she said, urgent. "We don't have long until we reach the station. We're running out of time."

"I'm fine," Leoni gasped. He pressed his back to the wall and began to slide down, his eyes flitting around the compartment, fixing on everything except for the body in the center of the room. Leoni's ice pack in his sock had graduated from mere droplets and was now leaking water onto the floor. A small puddle quickly formed beneath his sodden shoe.

"All right," Adele said. "Be safe. Call if you need anything."

Leoni made a shooing gesture toward both of them, reaching down and probing gingerly at his ankle. "I'll be fine, you go. Hurry."

Adele winced sympathetically, but felt a sudden jolt of anxiety and turned, with John moving after her. To her surprise, though, the Frenchman hesitated, and then, muttering darkly, stomped back toward where Leoni was resting.

"Here, use your sock, wrap it around the ice, and get some

124

compression on your ankle. Elevate it as well; take off your shoe, if you can, and place your heel on it."

Leoni looked up, surprised, as John, despite his gruff tone, very gently removed the Italian's shoe from his injured foot. He then placed it beneath the man's heel, gauging how much pain Leoni was in by how clenched his teeth seemed to go. John's demeanor was rough, but his hands moved like the cajoling fingers of a mother tending her young. His motions were efficient, still, rapid, and clearly conscious of passing time. Adele stared. John was a strange man—she'd always known it, but he always surprised her regardless.

Once Leoni's ankle was elevated and the Italian seemed settled, John got quickly back to his feet and began striding past Adele.

"Thanks," Adele murmured.

"We're wasting time," the Frenchman growled, "hurry up."

Adele didn't need a second invitation. She spared one last look toward her Italian friend, making sure he wasn't in too much pain; his head was now leaning back, the sweat on his face dripping down to his chin. But, at least for now, his eyes were closed, and he seemed to be breathing steadily, trying to focus on something besides the numb sensations.

She muttered darkly, and then moved after John through the first-class compartment, onto the sleeper cars, and toward the back, where the dormitory was.

As they hastened together, Adele could feel the wheels of the train shaking through the floorboards. As if, somehow, it was a ticking clock, threatening each passing moment. Was it her imagination? Or were they slowing? Maybe the conductor had decided to help a bit after all. But they didn't have time either way—they were almost at the station.

She pushed through the door into the staff dormitory. Inside, a couple of employees in waiter uniforms were staring up with a glazed look at a TV. Behind a veiled curtain, there were three bunks set in the wall.

"Johnson," Adele said, wishing now she had managed to snag a first name. "The reserve conductor, where is he?" she demanded.

The waiter and waitress leaning back on the couch blinked, startled, and one of them began to protest, "Hey, you're not supposed to be back—"

"It's the feds," the other one whispered, cutting him off. The girl said, "He's over there. Sleeping. He's not going to be happy if you

125

wake—"

But she didn't managed to finish her sentence either, before Adele and John rushed past, pushing through the veiled curtain and moving into the sleeping quarters with the three cots. The area was sparse, and Adele's gaze landed on a small lump beneath a thin blanket.

She reached out, suddenly finding her fingers trembling. The blanket wasn't moving. The lump seemed strangely motionless. Her heart began to hammer. She felt a strong sense of foreboding rising in her gut. "John," she said, her voice trembling.

Agent Renee stepped next to her, one hand on his hip, his eyes fixed on the motionless form beneath the blankets.

"Conductor," Adele said. "Johnson," she said, louder now.

She could feel the eyes of the two other staff fixed on her, and her shoulder blades itched. She reached out now and grabbed the arm beneath the blanket and shook the man. The body went limp and fell toward her. For a moment, her chest locked up, and her hands went still.

But then, suddenly, as if roused from a deep reverie, the conductor beneath the blanket jolted. He sat suddenly upright, gasping and cursing. The man's head collided with Adele's elbow, and just as quickly as he'd sprung up, he rebounded back, his head flopping onto the thin pillow.

"What on earth," he said, muttering, his voice creaking from a lack of sleep.

"Johnson," John said, shouting, "stay still, stop moving."

This, Adele decided, might not have been the best instruction for a man who was already motionless, with two looming shadows staring down at his sleeping form. The moment John's voice echoed out, it was clear Johnson realized he didn't recognize them. His eyes widened in fright, and his hands gripped the edge of the blanket, as if preparing to use it like a shield. He struggled away, sliding on his back and kicking with his feet to wedge up against the corner of the cot as far from them as he could manage, which wasn't a long trip.

"Who are you?" the conductor shouted.

"Hands where I can see them," John returned, at the same volume.

"Careful," Adele said, hesitantly. "Mr. Johnson, I'm with DGSI, and I'm here to talk—"

"Get away from me—don't—get back!" he snapped. Then he started shouting, "Help! Help, I'm being robbed!"

Adele quickly held up her hands, releasing the blankets she'd been holding without realizing it, her fingers grazing against the fabric. She held her hands out in mock surrender, taking two quick steps back. John reluctantly followed suit. And for a moment, the light from the TV screen behind them no longer cast their shadows over the reserve conductor's face. The man had a fading hairline, combed over, and a cherubic nose which spoke of youth, but crow's-feet eyes that contradicted the nose. He blinked, still clearing his eyes and trying to come to. The moment he spotted how large John was, he quailed back again but then his gaze found Adele, and his brow furrowed. "DGSI?" His sleep-deprived brain caught up with her words. "What are you talking about? What do you want from me?"

"Sir, we need to ask you to get out of the bed, please."

The man, though, seemed hesitant, some of the original fear creeping back into his posture, his eyes narrowed now. He held the blanket up over him, as if protecting himself in a cocoon against imminent attack.

"Were you on the LuccaRail?" John said, cutting to the chase, his shadow larger, and more foreboding than Adele's as it stretched from the light of TV across the small cot.

"Yes," the reserve conductor said, hesitantly. "But what does that have—"

"Yesterday were you a second on the Normandie Express?"

He frowned now. "I was, but I got *here* about eight hours ago. What does that—"

"Sir," Adele said, "were you aware there were dead bodies on both those trains?"

Now, the man was shaking his head, and it wasn't the only part of him trembling. His hands clutching the fabric of the blanket were turning white past the knuckles, and his cheeks went a similar hue. "Hang on just a moment," he said, hurriedly. "Are you implying that I had anything to do with that? Those were heart attacks. Two heart attacks. It's just a coincidence. You've got to be joking."

"Get out of bed," John said, sharply.

"You better listen, Johnson," shouted a voice from near the couch, as the waiter and waitress were now watching the events closer than they'd been staring at the TV. "The big one tried to punch Martha."

"I did not," John growled. "I don't even know who that is. Shut up," he added, pointing a thick finger behind the privacy curtain.

127

But the words from the waiter watching TV seemed to have their effect on Mr. Johnson. He continued to shake and tremble, and refused to rise from his cot. "Please," he was saying. "I have a family. A wife, two kids. Look, my wallet; I have a picture of them. Don't hurt me. I wasn't—"

"We're not here to hurt you," Adele said, firmly. She could feel her mind spinning. A competing swell of emotions, which included sympathy, frustration, and worry clashed with the evidence. This man had been a second on all three trains where the bodies were found. The only common staff among them. She set her jaw and said, "Please rise from the bed. We just need to talk. Do you have any belongings here?"

"It's just a coincidence," he murmured, his voice frail. "Two heart attacks. I know, strange. But it's just a coincidence."

"Sir, there have been *three* heart attacks. Another one on this train. You just so happen to have arrived directly before the murder."

The man's fingers went stiff. The blanket fell from his grip, tumbling onto his lap and revealing a sleeping T-shirt with stains as if from wine. "You're joking," he said, his eyes wide.

Again, Adele's emotions competed with her intellect. She knew psychopaths could act. They were tactical liars who perfected the craft over a lifetime of deceit. But also people telling the truth behaved in a similar way. The shock, the surprise, the note of tremor in his tone. All of it tugged on her heartstrings. But the cold hard facts competed. Three trains, three countries, three murders. Exactly one common point among them. She stared at him and his wine-stained white T-shirt.

"Get up," she said, firmly. "Now."

When the man continued to refuse to comply, John growled, reached out, and grabbed the man's wrist. As if he'd been shot, Johnson shouted suddenly and began kicking, trying to keep John back. "Get off me, get off!"

"What are you doing to him!" shouted one of the waiters.

"None of your business," John retorted. "Get up!" he bellowed. He yanked hard at the man's wrist.

The second conductor was pulled sharply from the bed, and sent stumbling to the ground. He was wearing sweatpants. His head nearly collided with the wall on the opposite side.

"Abuse!" shouted the waiter. "They're attacking Johnson!"

No one else seemed to hear the shouts, though. "I'm recording," the waitress screamed, and Adele glimpsed a black device lifted, aimed toward where John was standing over the fallen form of the trembling conductor.

"Put that away," Adele said, beseeching.

In response, the woman pointed the phone at Adele, now jutting her chin out defiantly. "You can't just go around doing whatever you want," the woman snapped. "You just threw him to the ground. He didn't do anything!"

"He killed three people," John retorted, snarling. "You're too stupid to realize maybe he would've attacked *you* next! The last victim was your age!"

The woman gasped in shock, now aiming the camera at John, as if she were flashing a middle finger.

Vaguely, Adele remembered John's track record with cameras, and in her mind's eye she glimpsed a particularly horrible event where a camera crew's equipment had been tossed off the edge of a cliff. Wincing, Adele quickly stepped between John and the recording woman. She held out a placating hand toward her partner, whose own hands were at his side, fingers clenched as if preparing to rip something to pieces.

"Calm down," she said, firmly. "Calm down."

John stared at her, his eyes blazing. In the past, whenever she placed herself between John and a terrible decision, he often listened, if only reluctantly. Now, though, he seemed at war. It seemed to take an extra amount of self-will to listen to her. Had things really gotten so cold between them? Didn't he care anymore what she thought?

At last, John spat, turned, and stomped over to the corner of the dormitory car. One large hand reached out and began rummaging through a duffel bag, which had been crammed in the side cabinet next to the beds.

"You don't have permission to go through that!" the reserve conductor was saying, shouting from where he was still sitting on the floor. He was massaging his elbow, and wincing, but he was at least no longer trembling as he stared at John's back.

Adele approached the fallen man, saying, "I'm sorry. Please, if everyone could just calm down. We do need to speak with you though."

The conductor stared up at her, seemingly emboldened by the camera pointed in his direction. "I didn't do anything," he snapped. "You're insane. Why are you even here?"

"Sir, think of it from my perspective. You're the only one who was at all three crime scenes. Moving crime scenes, I might add. Not exactly easy to sneak in and out."

He shrugged. "I don't know anything about that. Heart attacks happen all the time. It's one of the leading causes of death." He spoke in a condescending way that made Adele feel her own temper rising.

"Get out of there," Johnson shouted, toward John's back.

But the large Frenchman didn't seem in the mood to listen. He continued to rummage around, tossing clothing items over his shoulder. A pair of boxers landed across Mr. Johnson's knee, draping over his leg.

Adele could feel the camera still poking toward them.

She sighed. She'd forgotten how frustrating it could be to work with John sometimes. He was a competent shooter, an excellent protector. But his ability to communicate with others without infuriating them was nearly impossible. She remembered how he'd tried to tend to Agent Leoni's injured leg. At the same time, not everyone was in a boot camp. He was acting like the conductor was nothing more than a rookie in a military squadron. Civilians didn't take kindly to that sort of manhandling.

"John, maybe we should—" she began, but before she could finish, John declared, "Aha!"

He whirled around. A snarl was in his voice, as he jutted an item toward Mr. Johnson. "What is this?" he declared, emphasizing the last word with a dramatic flourish.

Adele's own protest was caught mid-sentence. She stared at the item in John's hand, and went suddenly cold. In a clear plastic bag, she spotted a syringe—the sort of shot one might use to apply a toxin. Next to the shot, a thin bottle with clear liquid.

The shot and the unmarked bottle were both in a plastic bag. John wiggled it, aiming it in the direction of the seated conductor. "Well?" he said, sternly. "Mind explaining this? If you're so innocent."

The conductor gasped for a moment, shaking his head from side to side and stumbling a bit. For the first time, the waitress's camera seemed to be centered on the item in John's hand, rather than the Frenchman himself. At least this seemed a small mercy.

"My insulin," said Mr. Johnson, stuttering now. "You're going through my things. You shouldn't do that. You're not even allowed."

"I'm allowed," John snorted. "Take it up with the judge. You expect me to believe this is insulin? How come there are no markings?"

"I had to move it to another bottle," the conductor said, quickly. His eyes widened, and his tone became high-pitched. Adele realized he was beginning to panic. Was it because he knew he was guilty? Or because he knew how it looked to have a bottle and a syringe, while being accused of causing heart attacks in three victims? Was that guilt? Or fear? Or both?

"I'm diabetic," the man said, shivering. "The insulin is normally marked. But this one I had to move to a new bottle after the other one broke. I didn't have time to get a new prescription. I was going on a ten-day trip, before heading home."

"Sir," Adele said, slowly, staring at the bottle and the syringe, "I'm afraid you need to come with us." The man in his wine-stained shirt and soft sweatpants was shaking again. He turned toward the camera directed at him, pleading, "Please, I didn't do anything."

But now, even the waitress and the waiter who'd been jeering from the back were staring stonily toward where the conductor crouched. The camera was facing him, recording, and the conductor sighed, shaking his head, his shoulders slumping.

Then, as John lowered the bag, Mr. Johnson, in a surprising show of speed suggesting he'd been playing up just how frightened he was, surged to his feet and bolted past Adele, racing rapidly away.

John cursed and lunged, but missed.

Adele was knocked back, an elbow shoved into her chest, and she stumbled, nearly tripping over another duffel bag which had been left next to the privacy screen separating the cots from the TV.

Mr. Johnson raced forward, sprinting toward the divider in the back of the dormitory car.

"Stop!" Adele shouted.

John, having recovered first, jammed the insulin bottle into Adele's arms and sprinted after the retreating form. His long legs covered the distance rapidly, his footsteps thumping into the ground. John flung himself into the air. The waitress must've had a degree in filming, because she didn't seem to miss anything. She tracked with her video camera as John hurtled, parallel to the floor, arms outstretched.

Adele watched in slow motion, it seemed, as John slammed into the back of the reserve conductor and brought him crashing down to the ground in a pile of limbs.

Mr. Johnson let out a croaking sob, and John scrambled on top, holding him firmly to the ground, both hands placed in the smaller

131

man's back. "Don't move," John barked. "Stay down. Don't move. Stay on the ground."

Adele, massaging her chest where she'd been elbowed, held the bag with the shot and the unknown substance, delicately keeping it at arm's length as she moved across the dormitory car, toward the collapsed forms of the two men.

After another couple of curses and a flurry of struggling, Mr. Johnson went limp, and his voice probed out in the suddenly still car. "I want to call my lawyer."

CHAPTER TWENTY EIGHT

Mr. Johnson sat glumly in the remodeled car, shooting the occasional look of reproach toward where the body lay beneath the tarp. "I want to speak with the real police," he muttered, darkly. "You're not even German! Let me go!"

John turned and snapped, "Quiet. We're almost to the station, then you can have your precious German police take you to prison."

The man muttered a series of dark oaths beneath his breath, one hand raised, cuffed to a metal rail next to one of the bare walls.

"How much longer, do you think?" Adele asked quietly beneath her breath, addressing Agent Leoni, where he fiddled with his phone, tracking their progress on GPS.

"Five or so minutes, tops," Leoni murmured, raising his eyes to look at the glaring reserve conductor.

"Why should it matter?" John called across the car, making no effort to lower his voice. His large frame blockaded the glass partition into first class, preventing any prying eyes. "We have the bastard." He nodded toward Mr. Johnson. John had a couple of scrape marks along one cheek and a pretty bruise just beneath his eye.

Adele winced in sympathy, but John noticed the gesture and only glowered even more.

She sighed, passing a hand through her hair and reminding herself to take a shower first opportunity she got. Still, as she felt the train continue to rumble beneath them, she couldn't shake the rising feeling of unease somewhere in her gut.

It all seemed off, somehow…

She regarded Mr. Johnson, feeling a dash of sympathy again. He took a long sip from the water bottle she'd managed to finagle from the valet and his cart. She figured it was the least she could have done, given how things had gone back in the dormitory car.

"I don't know…" she murmured, glancing at John, then returning to look at Mr. Johnson.

"Don't know?" Renee said. "Don't know what, Agent Sharp? He's the guy. You saw the poison yourself."

133

"It might be insulin, though."

"You're buying that? He resisted arrest!"

"We did catch him while sleeping. And you weren't exactly nice about it."

John snorted, crossing his arms and slouching against the glass partition at his back. "He was on all three trains where a victim was murdered. His name wasn't on the manifest."

"Yes, but the manifest wasn't his doing. Remember what the conductor said? They sometimes don't even mark down the seconds."

"Still," John said, shrugging his large shoulders. "It has to be him." He turned to regard Leoni. "What do you think, hmm? Is this the guy?" Again, John made no effort to lower his voice, and Mr. Johnson pretended to be particularly interested in the floor all of a sudden. Adele guessed he was listening to every word—she wasn't sure if he was French, but to travel as much as he did and work on French trains, he likely knew the language.

Leoni, in perfect French, replied, "I don't know." He looked apologetically up at Adele. "It does fit, a bit. He could be lying about the insulin."

"I'm not!" Johnson called.

"Quiet!" Renee retorted.

Adele felt another flash of unease. "But what motive?" she said, lowering her voice even more and turning her back fully to the man in custody. "Why would he kill travelers—it makes no sense."

"He's insane," John said simply, finally—to her relief—matching her volume.

Adele paused, clicking her tongue, lost in thought. The motive simply wasn't there. He'd had the means, the opportunity, but *why?* It wasn't like anyone else fit the bill. They had no other suspects. No one else on the staff manifest or passenger list who'd been on all three trains. Why kill wealthy first-class passengers in three separate countries? Besides, as a reserve conductor, he wouldn't even have interacted with them. How could he have poisoned them?

The killer would have a reason, a gripe, a grudge. Some hidden hatred. And while Johnson seemed particularly loathsome of Agent Renee at this moment, it wasn't like he didn't have cause. She hadn't detected any other motive. So far, all he'd done was deny and shout for a lawyer.

No motive, then.

So why kill?

"I don't know," Adele murmured, quietly. "I don't think it's him."

At that moment, a voice suddenly echoed off the intercom, reverberating in the still room. "We are now approaching our final destination. Please stay away from the doors until we've come to a complete stop. Thank you for your patience during this delay. In addition, we'd like to offer any passengers who want to travel with us in the coming month a deal for half off their next ticket in way of a thank-you for your continued patience."

The voice crackled over the speakers and then went silent.

Adele shifted uncomfortably, staring at the black speakers above the windows. Soon, they'd be disembarking. There was no more time. But there was also no motive. No time left to find another suspect.

"Excuse me," she said, suddenly, looking across at Mr. Johnson.

He stopped studying the floor long enough to glance up and present her with a scowl. "What?"

"I'm sorry for any inconvenience, truly. Things..." she half glanced toward John, but returned her gaze to Mr. Johnson, "may have gotten a bit out of hand."

He jangled the handcuff against the rail, waving his one hand. "You think so, do you?"

"Look, I'm sorry," she said, firmly. "But please understand, we're trying to catch a serial murderer. Three people have died, and we're running out of time. The killer is on this train, right now."

John interjected, "And you're speaking to him right now."

"Maybe so," Adele continued, picking up speed. "But if you maintain your innocence," she addressed the reserve conductor, "then I need your help with something."

"My help?" he asked, somehow conveying a snort in the two short words.

"Yes. The deaths, they occurred on the three trains you've been on. All of them in a different country."

"And?"

"And," she pressed, "is there anything else we might be missing about the location? We've already had a death in Germany... But... But I can't shake the notion that the killer might strike again." She frowned, shaking her head. Then, more to herself than anyone, she murmured, "We've been operating under the assumption the killer is attacking one per country, and once per day... but what if we were

135

wrong about that?" She looked at Mr. Johnson. "Is there anything else you might have seen? You were on the first two trains. You're on this one."

"I told you already," he snapped. "I didn't even know someone had died."

"Ridiculous," John said. "Adele, come on now. He's playing you. Don't listen to him."

The conductor seemed caught between his anger with John and the lifeline Adele had just tossed him. It took him a moment to consider, but then he said, "When?"

"Excuse me?" Adele asked.

"When did the victim die?"

"The woman—Margaret," said John. "She had a name, you know."

"Most of us do," the conductor retorted. "When did she die?"

Adele said, "About four hours ago. Is that relevant?"

"Four hours? Just after we crossed into West Germany? In the Black Forest, yes?"

Adele hesitated. "I think so, yes."

The conductor shrugged. "Well, there you have it. Another switch."

"Excuse me?"

"A switch," he said. "A rail shift. The first two deaths occurred right before or right after a switch in the tracks."

Adele stared, feeling her lips go suddenly numb. For a moment, she felt a prickle along her back, and she swallowed. "A switch? You're sure?"

"I noticed it with the first two heart attacks. Didn't know they were murders. Some of the wait staff thought the switches were cursed." He shrugged. "We all noticed, though. It's at the switches these people are dying."

Adele looked off out the window. She could see buildings now, see streets and alleys as they pulled closer to the train station. Soon, the killer would be able to slip away. Without a controlled environment, his escape seemed imminent. But this new theory... the switches? Could that be it? Was the killer somehow connected to the track changes?

"The next switch," Adele said, suddenly. "When is it?"

Mr. Johnson paused for a moment, his eyes narrowing as he examined her. Then his gaze flitted down to the water bottle she'd given him. He looked determinedly away from John, as if intent on ignoring the Frenchman. And, with a sigh, the reserve conductor said,

136

"Just past this station, actually. We're rolling up on one right now."

CHAPTER TWENTY NINE

Adele could feel the train chugging along beneath her, but with it came a rising sense of anxiety to match. She turned to John, her mouth numb with the words cajoled from her lips. "I... I don't think it's him."

John rolled his eyes. "Adele, come on," he insisted. "Of course it is. Look at him. He was on all three trains. He attacked me. He has the toxin."

"You attacked me, and it's insulin!" Johnson called.

"I don't think it's him," Adele repeated, in a whisper. "And I might be wrong, but if I'm right about him, then the killer is going to strike again, very soon."

"You're buying this crap about the switches?"

"It makes sense, doesn't it?"

"Not coming from him, it doesn't," John said, jutting his chin.

"John," Adele said softly. "I know we haven't seen eye to eye lately... But can you trust me on this one? I've been right before."

At these words, John hesitated. His expression seemed set in stone, but as she held his gaze, a light almost seemed to flicker behind his eyes, and his countenance morphed, slowly, and his eyes softened. He gave a half nod and muttered, "On your head be it..."

"Fine. I'll take all the blame. Just, please, this once...*trust me*."

John hesitated, but then his shoulders sagged. He shrugged. "You've been right before. If I can't convince you, then fine. So what do we do? We're already pulling in."

Leoni looked up from where he'd collapsed on his ankle. "I can look after the conductor," he said, wincing. "If Adele's right..."

The two DGSI agents looked at the Italian and nodded slowly.

John, though, if only to underscore his point, gestured out the window. Adele could even hear the screech of the train against the tracks as it began to come to a full stop. Out of time. Any moment now, the killer would make good his getaway. She had to make a call—they didn't have time to search the train again. No time to look through all the cars.

A final shot in the dark—she had to pick a target.

"First class," she murmured. "He'll be near the victims. He's killed three wealthy folk already—he'll do it again. And we're nearing the switch," she said and glanced toward Mr. Johnson. "If what he says is correct... First class," Adele said at last. "We have to go, come."

She turned and began moving away from the body beneath the tarp, and the reserve conductor chained to the rail. John, for his part, didn't seem so reluctant anymore. It wasn't that he liked being bossed around. Adele knew, however, that if there was one thing she could rely on John for, it was that he would have her back. No matter what. Even if he disagreed. For all his sharp edges and unconventional methods, he was loyal to the end.

She could feel him moving next to her now, striding toward the glass partition that led to first class.

Just then, all of a sudden, everything went black for a moment. Adele fell still, stunned. A brief passing thought suggested she'd fallen unconscious. But she could still feel the train shaking beneath her, and could even hear John's breathing at her side. A second passed, then another, and then the train emerged from the darkness, light streaking the windows at her side once more.

"What was that?" Adele said, frowning.

"A weather sheath," said the conductor. "It's a tunnel. There's going to be another one before you finally come to a—"

"It's going to go dark like that again?"

Johnson, though, seemed bored with answering all these questions, and was now plucking at the handcuff around his wrist.

Adele could feel the train slowing nearly completely now. If they passed through another one of these makeshift weather-protection tunnels, time would be up. Already, the killer, if he was bold, could try to escape by hopping off the slowly moving train and disappearing into the city.

Now was the time for boldness in return.

With John at her side, she shoved into the first-class compartment, shaking off the sudden shock of the darkened train car.

The whistle of scraping wheels against the track was soon replaced by the quiet mutter of voices in the first-class compartment. People sat in the chairs facing the windows, while others sat in the cushioned seats, sipping from wineglasses or poking at snacks brought to them on the trolley.

"What are we looking for?" John pressed, his voice low.

Adele answered honestly. "I don't know yet. Just keep your eyes peeled."

They stood at the front of the first-class car, and Adele could feel the eyes of the passengers fixed on her. She glanced around, surveying the passengers. For a moment, her gaze landed on the old man by the window. The one who had often smiled when she'd come through. He had a strange way about him. His eyes would always track her, when he didn't think she was watching. She began to move toward him, but then heard a sudden spark of laughter. Her eyes darted toward where Richard and Bella, the two friends of the third victim, were chuckling to each other and muttering beneath their voices as they pointed toward some other woman sitting in the back of the car. For two friends who had lost a loved one, they sure didn't seem too broken up about it. Adele now took a step toward them.

And just then, she heard a grumble from the back of the compartment. The woman who'd been the subject of Richard and Bella's derision was arguing with the valet, trying to exchange a pack of opened peanuts, it seemed, for pretzels.

The valet looked flustered, and was shaking his head.

The woman with the peanuts flung them at the valet, and a few of the nuts bounced off his red uniform.

For a moment, the valet's countenance darkened. Gone was the bumbling, stuttering young man. Gone was the timid, frightful staff member, wanting nothing more than to be left alone. For a moment, Adele glimpsed a snarl twist the valet's lips. The young man didn't look so young anymore. Maybe she'd been wrong about twenty. Maybe mid-twenties. He had a boyish face, but there was nothing innocent about the look of sheer loathing twisting his features now as he regarded the woman who'd thrown the peanuts. One hand was trembling as it reached toward the pretzels the woman had demanded. But it wasn't trembling from fear or embarrassment. His knuckles were pale, with the white fury of sheer rage. Adele stared, rooted to the floor, feeling John brush past her as he moved slowly along the first-class cabin, glancing at the passengers on either side. But Adele only had eyes for the valet.

He'd said he'd heard a noise. He'd said it had been a crash. The old man had corrected him.

At the time, Adele had wondered if perhaps she'd missed a clue. But now, what if he'd been simply trying to throw her off? To confuse

140

the investigation? But why would he want to do that?

She stared at him, watching as he shoved the pretzels into the hand of the peanut-flinging woman.

Then, slowly, as if sensing the attention, the valet's eyes shifted away from the woman in the back of the first-class car. He looked slowly up, his head rotating, tilting, and his eyes suddenly settled on Adele's. For a moment, they stared across the cabin. None of the other first-class residents seemed to notice. Not even John seemed to spot the interchange. Adele could feel her breath coming slow. She was staring into the eyes of someone she didn't recognize. She'd had a conversation with the valet. Had interviewed him. But something else was now staring back at her. Something she didn't fully recognize. The sheer hatred, the loathing that had flashed across his face for that brief glimpse, wasn't so brief after all. She could see it now, etched deep, carved into the core of his eyes. Not a light, not a glow, but a stony, frigid fixture. A hatred so bone deep that it cut through anything else that might have been displayed in the windows to the soul.

And she was staring right at it. The valet didn't look away at first. And then, as if suddenly breaking from a reverie, he seemed to realize who was looking back at him. He glanced down and rearranged some of the peanuts, shifting his head a bit and glancing sheepishly side to side. But the effect of the mirage was failing now. He was trying to play dumb. Trying to play timid. But the church mouse had already revealed itself to be a wolf. She wouldn't fall for it again.

And so she didn't look away. She knew.

And as she stared at him and began to pick up her pace, marching across the first-class compartment, he knew too. She could see the recognition dawning in his eyes. Could see the realization of the futility of pretense. He stopped rearranging the glistening packets of peanuts, and instead stared right back at her. One of his hands crept into his pocket, and Adele's own went to her hip.

"Sharp?" John said, suddenly, as if noting something in her posture.

"It's him," Adele said, breathlessly.

And then they entered another tunnel. The train was scraping along in the station. And suddenly, everything went dark. Mr. Johnson, the reserve conductor, had warned there would be another one of these weather tunnels. But now, in the pitch-black, Adele lost sight of the valet. She cursed, feeling the cold of her weapon in her hand as she pulled it out. But there was nothing to aim at. It had been daytime, with sunlight through the windows, which meant no other sources of light were illuminating the inside of the now darkened train.

"Adele?" said the disembodied voice of John in her ear.

"The valet," she hissed. "It's the valet."

And then, she heard movement. The sound of a rolling cart. It seemed to be picking up speed. She could barely pick it out over the squeal of the train against the tracks. She could barely pick it out over the sound of her own haggard breathing. But there it was, a whirring sound, a blurring motion she could barely glimpse, reflected, for the briefest instant, off the glow of someone's phone in the middle aisle.

"Your reading lights," Adele shouted, suddenly. "Turn your reading lights on, now!"

The train was moving at a molasses pace, prolonging the time spent in the weather tunnel just outside the station.

For a moment no one responded, and now she could hear the thumping of footsteps, the whirring of the cart as it came forward, careening down the aisle.

And then the old man with the smiling face responded first. He reached up and flicked on a light. Suddenly, the low glow of orange illuminated the faintest portion of the train car. Most of the first class was still bathed in dark, but the shadows were pushed back, and light intercepted the careening snack cart. A large metal box was zipping toward them, pushed by the valet. He had a ferocious glare affixed to his face. His teeth gritted together. One hand was pushing the cart, but the other had something he had pulled from his pocket. Adele glimpsed a flash of a needle. Another reading light turned on, and it illuminated the item in the man's hand. A syringe. A third reading light turned on, now seemingly tracking the progress of the wheeling valet.

And then he was on them. He released another enormous shout, howling as he surged toward them. "Die!"

CHAPTER THIRTY

John, suddenly noting the trajectory of the cart, and noting Adele was directly in the path of the careening chunk of metal on wheels, moved first with a shout, lunging forward. Adele hadn't been idle, either, though, and was quickly moving, trying to put herself between the seats, to shield herself from the cart. But Richard and Bella, the two friends of Margaret, were caught up with each other, and as Adele pressed near them for shelter, Richard grunted and stiff-armed her, shoving her away and saying, "Get off me."

Adele was sent back out into the aisle. John, seeing this, cursed. He lurched forward, grabbed at Adele, and pushed her bodily on top of Richard. At the same time, this brought John into direct contact with the surging cart. It slammed into his hip and sent the tall Frenchman toppling over it. John yelled in pain as he went flying, rolling across a pile of peanuts and water bottles, and then flipped over the other side. The Frenchman, despite the sudden motion, tried to snag at the valet's shoulder.

But he missed. The slight form of the young staff member moved quickly and then reached out and flipped off two of the lights that had already been turned on. Again, darkness filled the cabin. One light at the very back of the compartment illuminated where John had fallen, groaning, trying to push back to his feet after getting pounded by a ton of wheeled metal and snacks. For her part, Adele desperately cried, "Turn on your lights!"

But the valet was quick, and he turned off the final reading light.

Now, the passengers seemed confused. On one hand, they heard a shouted instruction from someone who claimed to be a federal agent from France. On the other, someone in an actual uniform, one of the staff members they were familiar with, was flipping off their lights. And so, fear and uncertainty seemed to stay their hands. And again, darkness swallowed them.

"Just die," the valet sneered, his voice like oil, slick and anxious.

Adele's own weapon moved about, but again, in the dark, it was impossible to aim until she suddenly felt a hand grip her wrist.

She cursed, struggling, bumping against the cart that had sent her partner flying. She heard more shouting. She felt a hand shove at her again, and Richard's voice, "Get off me!"

She gritted her teeth, resisting the urge to reach out and slap at Bella's boyfriend. She needed her full attention now fixed on the unseen form of the valet. She heard a quiet huffing and desperate breaths as he struggled, trying to grip her wrist and push her away. At the same time, she remembered what she'd spotted in his other hand. She couldn't see the syringe now, moving about somewhere in the dark.

In her mind's eye, she pictured a presumed trajectory. She'd tangled with knife-wielding suspects before. They always stabbed a certain way. The valet couldn't sweep in an arcing fashion, as the seats around him would prevent the motion. So his hand would be above, stabbing downward.

Lobbing a desperate prayer, she raised her own forearm, her one hand still gripped by the wrist, but the other free to maneuver in a blocking motion.

And suddenly, something firm slammed against her upraised forearm. Bone clashed against bone. She heard a grunt of pain. For a moment, she listened, hoping to hear the clatter of the syringe. But the valet was strong, and he didn't seem to lose his grip.

She cursed and lashed out, kicking. She'd been aiming for his legs, but missed, and instead, in the dark, kicked the trolley.

He was too close now for her to shoot. He gripped the wrist of her hand holding the firearm. She tried to aim, but it was impossible. The gun was pointed up toward the ceiling.

"Just die," he screamed. "You killed him. And so you die."

Adele didn't know what he was talking about. But if he was talking, it meant he was distracted from stabbing. And so, grunting, and heaving a breath of exertion, she gasped, "Who? I didn't do anything. Stop moving!"

"You killed him! You made him suffer, and you killed him!"

And then the young man tried to reach for her neck, releasing his grip on her forearm. She moved her hand with the gun. Another reading light switched on, this time again from the old man.

Adele cursed as the valet realized his mistake. He spotted the firearm, and suddenly pushed her hand back again. Again, the weapon was pointed toward the ceiling.

Just beyond, Adele spotted John grunting and rising. He was

bleeding from a gash over his forehead, a jagged cut along his forearm. In pain and injured, he saw Adele's plight, and with a growl bodily flung himself over the snack car, trying to reach her.

But he was moving slowly, encumbered by his injuries, and Adele glimpsed the syringe. The reading light from the old man showed the syringe next to Adele's neck. A needle was jabbing toward her. She could feel it scrape against her shoulder, just missing.

She didn't know what sort of toxin he'd used. But it had killed three people. Just an inch away. A fraction of an inch. If she wasn't careful, she'd be next. What could she do, though? Her hands were tied up. They were locked in their struggle. The needle was in his grip, more deadly than her gun in such close proximity.

And suddenly, the train emerged from the weather tunnel and came to a final, scraping halt. It was a climactic moment of motion. Everything went still. Light suddenly flooded through the train again. Another voice announced something over the black speakers above the windows. But this time, Adele couldn't hear what it was saying, as she was too focused on the needle, now against her neck. She could feel it pressing, feel it practically nip against her skin. The needle suddenly jabbed in, hard, and she cursed.

She'd released her grip on his forearm. But intentionally.

The needle wasn't the threat. It was the contents inside the shot itself. And while the needle was in her neck. He hadn't yet pushed the plunger. She grabbed the edge of the shot, pressing her thumb directly between the plunger and the stem of the shot.

The valet cursed, trying to inject the toxin, but failing. With the needle in her neck, as close to death as she'd ever been, Adele fired her gun.

Once, twice.

Still aiming at the ceiling. Still without any sort of trajectory on the killer himself.

But she didn't need it to be. The gun was next to his ear. It fired, and Adele jerked her head back as she did, aware of just how loud the thing could be in close quarters.

The valet suddenly shouted in pain—the flash of the muzzle, the horrific blast directly next to his left ear. He screamed, and suddenly, his hand went limp. Adele yanked the plunger from his grip, and pulled the needle from her neck.

She lashed out with the butt of the gun, slamming it into the bridge of the valet's nose. He took a couple of stumbling steps back; blood erupted from his nose and poured down his lips.

For a moment, he stood there, and they were no longer in the dark. The train was at a full stop. And the valet stood in front of the snack cart he'd used as a battering ram, one hand clutched to his ear, the other shaking and trembling where he'd dropped the syringe. Blood flowed freely down his nose. He stared at Adele, wide-eyed, stammering, and shook his head. "I don't, I didn't—"

And then Agent John Renee tackled him full force from behind. The valet's head snapped back, and he was sent crashing to the ground with all of John's muscular frame behind him, bringing him to a thumping halt against the floor of the train car.

John looked up, holding the man down, still bleeding from the gash in his forehead and the injury to his forearm. Gasping heavily, he looked at Adele. "I got it," he said. "You're safe, I got it."

Adele resisted a strange, inexplicable urge to grin. "Yeah, you did it," she said.

She could still feel the pain in her neck where the needle had jammed. She gripped the syringe she'd ripped from his hand. Her other hand went slowly limp, and she placed her weapon back in its holster. She glanced up, spotting two bullet holes, which had punctured the ceiling of the train car, allowing more light to flood through even such small gaps.

"Good job," she said to John.

And this time, still bleeding, and yet not seeming to care, John returned her grin, flashing teeth. He glanced down at the valet and snapped, "Stop it. You're done. Just stop."

And the young valet stopped struggling, and he began to cry, shaking against the ground and cursing at Adele, at John, and anyone who looked in his direction.

CHAPTER THIRTY ONE

Adele regarded the train which had come to a complete halt beneath the shelter of the station at last. Shaken passengers disembarked, some of them glancing around as if shell-shocked, others—especially the ones who'd been in the first-class compartment—leaning on each other, or conversing in hushed whispers. Ticket collectors and attendants hastily guided the passengers to other trains to complete their trips.

Adele turned and exited the station, feeling a lightness to her step that hadn't been there before. By an SUV, John and Leoni were talking to an officer, using the Italian to translate the Frenchman to the German. Adele just glimpsed the hunched silhouette of the young valet in the back of the SUV.

She winced, reaching up and probing at her neck where he'd jabbed his needle. So close to death—there would have been nothing the others could do. They still didn't completely know the origin of the toxin, but they'd found another bottle of the substance in the valet's personal effects.

It hadn't taken long to convince John to release the relief conductor. As he'd left, he'd promised the tall Frenchman he'd be hearing from his lawyers. To Adele's surprise, John had actually attempted an apology—but it hadn't been well received.

Now, outside the German station, beneath the winking sun and folds of cloud, Adele moved across the sidewalk to the parking lot and approached the SUV with the suspect inside.

As she neared, she could still feel the lightness in her footsteps. For some reason, this troubled her.

She frowned, trying to place the sensation... Then she realized: what had been the source of the horrible foreboding? She'd felt certain this case would end terribly. Not so much a sixth sense, but a *feeling*. She didn't know what to make of it. The killer was in custody—no doubt about that. Three lives claimed, a tragedy, but not unusual in her line of work.

Adele picked up the pace, reaching the SUV.

She could her John muttering to Leoni beneath his breath, "Let him take the guy. Why should we? They're the ones who wanted to handle the case, aren't they?"

Leoni reluctantly translated in German, using more diplomatic language. The German officer in question sighed and shrugged.

Leoni spotted Adele and his countenance brightened. She gave a little wave, but then moved around the other side of the SUV, past the darkened glass. The silhouette within the vehicle went stiff all of a sudden as if noting this new attention.

For a moment, Adele paused outside the car, her hand hovering near the handle. They'd solved the case. She ought to let it go...

And yet, she still couldn't shake the strangest of feelings. She hated the sense of leaving something unfinished. Was there something she'd missed? Or were her emotions completely out of whack? To anyone else, it might have seemed like the vanity of perusing tea leaves in the bottom of cup. But Adele's instincts, like the senses of a bloodhound, had proved effective over the course of her entire career. Her instincts, which she couldn't always explain, had led to more than one arrest, more than one closed case.

So why, now, did it seem like her sense of impending doom, her sense of something cresting the horizon—why did it seem like she'd missed it?

Her fingers touched against the cool metal of the handle.

Let it go... she thought to herself.

But then, as she listened to John and Leoni continue to barter with the German officer, her eyes narrowed. "No," she said out loud to her own subconscious.

And then she grabbed the handle, pulled open the door, and slid into the back seat opposite the serial poisoner.

The young valet didn't look so frightening now, cuffed in the back seat, buckled against the cool glass and reclining on the door. His eyes roamed around the car for a moment, and then shifted to her—a sidelong glance of passing curiosity more than anything.

When the young man recognized her, his eyes widened a bit, and he turned, as much as he could in his restrained form, and acknowledged her with a blink.

Adele watched him, unblinking herself, her gaze fixed on the killer. And yet, to think of him in terms any less than "human" didn't seem to do justice. He was so young, so lost. She'd seen the hatred in his eyes, seen the loathing. Seen his complete and cold disregard for the lives of others. He'd tried to kill her, after all.

And yet, she couldn't shake a feeling of sympathy. A shared pain. For a moment, she had a sense as if she were staring into a reflection of a sort. She remembered losing her mother, just after turning twenty. It seemed so long ago now, but in the grand scheme of things, it was little more than a passing day.

"What do you want?" the valet asked at last, swallowing and staring.

Adele watched him a moment longer without responding. The other agents didn't seem to have noticed she'd entered the vehicle. This served her fine. She wanted some alone time with the killer—a few moments to simply chat.

"I don't know," she said, honestly, after a moment. Her earlier sense of foreboding had faded. Her worries, her fear, seemed to have vanished. Had she missed it? She frowned in thought, looking across his young features.

"How old are you?" she asked.

He grunted. "Twenty-five. It's in my ID."

She nodded slowly. Older than she'd first thought, but still young. "I... I don't normally do this," she said. "I know you probably won't want to tell me. The German authorities will likely want to question you themselves..."

"That's a lot of preamble," he muttered.

"I'll cut to it." Adele fixed her gaze on him once more. "Why did you do it?"

"Do what?" he said, belligerently.

"I'm not asking on the record. Confess or don't—it doesn't matter. The evidence is overwhelming against you. We double-checked the passenger and staff lists of the trains again, too. That's how we missed you the first time. You logged as a passenger on the LuccaRail. But as a staff member on Normandie Express." She nodded. "Clever."

"You can't sweet talk me," he retorted. He turned, obstinately staring out the window again.

"Fine," she said. "I can't get you to talk. Let me talk a little then." Adele continued to watch the killer, even though he'd turned away. She *needed* to know, now. Something wasn't adding up. She'd missed it. Maybe this business with her mother's killer reemerging had completely thrown her instincts off. Maybe she was losing it...

She frowned deeply at this final thought, and through pressed teeth said, "You truly hated them, didn't you? The first-class passengers? Was it their wealth? Their looks?"

"Looks?" he snorted. "You seen half of those ogres? No."

"So what then?"

"I told you, I'm not talking. Leave me alone."

"I'd like to. I lost my mother, you know…" Adele felt stunned by her own words. She had never voluntarily shared that with a killer before. She rarely shared it with friends. And yet the words tumbled from her lips, dragged—it seemed—again by instinct. She followed up with, "Was it your mother? Or your father?"

He turned to her again now, a haunted look in his gaze. "What?"

"That hatred," she said. "I recognized it because I've seen it before. Usually reflected in a mirror. I know the loss. I don't know why you blamed the passengers. But I know the feeling."

The killer reclined his head against the rest and shook his head firmly. "You don't know what you're talking about. You're lying."

"I'm not. My mother. Ten years ago. Butchered."

For a moment, she thought he might say something disparaging or dismissive. She wasn't sure she wouldn't slap him if he did. Sometimes John Renee's approach seemed the only path.

But instead, the valet just looked at her, his young features softening, if only a fraction. "That's awful," he said. "I'm sorry."

Adele went quiet, considering these words from a man who'd just killed three people. He seemed so… sincere. And yet the gulf between them—their choices—was nearly insurmountable. She refrained from speaking her thoughts, though, and dipped her head once to accept the conciliation. She waited, listening to the quiet breathing in the back of the police car. Listening to the thrum of muttered voices just outside the glass. Sometimes, listening was key.

After another passing minute, the young man glanced at her and muttered, "My father."

"Sorry," Adele replied on reflex.

The man shrugged, his cuffs shifting as he did in his lap, his forearms resting against his knees. "Never knew my mother. But my father and I were close, you know…"

"I know… How did it happen?"

The young man sighed. "Not like you won't be able to find out anyway."

"I told you, I'm not here to make a case. Not even recording. You

150

have my word."

"Your word? I'm going to prison, aren't I?"

"Probably for a very long time. I can't do anything about that. You killed three people."

"People?" he snorted again, his voice hardening. "Cockroaches," he said. "Parasites. All of them. They did it, you know," he continued, some of the previous fury flashing in his eyes. He began to build up a head of steam as he spoke, the words starting to come faster. "They killed him. All of them. The way they treated him—like dirt. He was a conductor, you know. He ran the same line…"

"The switches," Adele said. "Where you killed. That was your father's route?"

"Dunno," he said, with a sniff. But his eyes told the story.

"It was, wasn't it? Your father was a conductor, then. What happened?"

"Fired him—the company did. Some rich bastards complained. Said the ride was too bumpy or some shit. It's a goddamn train; of course it's bloody bumpy."

"That's why he got fired?"

"Well… maybe some other things. Made up things. A couple of the women said he made them uncomfortable—a damned lie, though! And another man said my father showed up drunk to the job. But that was only once! I swear it. Only once and they went and fired him. Stripped away the only thing that mattered to him. Left him broke, helpless, trying to raise me with nothing. All of the whiners, the complainers—all of them were rich assholes."

"They cost your father his job?"

He rounded fully on her now, his eyes blazing once more with hatred. "Cost him more than that!" he spat. "He got mad—got dangerous. Never was like that before. Not usually. Drank a ton. Gave me more than one scar."

"He beat you?"

The valet snorted again.

"Then what happened?"

He got in his truck," said the valet, murmuring now, his eyes staring off as if watching something a million miles away. "Drove to the tracks, parked in the middle. Late at night, raining. No chance for the conductor to see a thing."

"He killed himself?"

151

At this, the young man laughed. "Actually, no." There was no humor to the cackling sound. Just an abandoned, empty husk of a noise. An echo of joy more than the thing itself. "He died of a heart attack. That's what the coroner said. Got right up and terrified as the train came down. Heart attack took him right out before the train could. Car was crushed too. But the heart attack did him in."

Adele nodded slowly. "So that's why you killed them the way you did?"

"I never said that."

"No, I guess you didn't... Well, I'm sorry."

"Sorry enough to get me out of jail?"

"I'm not the one putting you there. You might not believe me, but I don't like to see people in your position... not unless they've made their own choices. And you did—three times. Almost a fourth."

The valet glanced toward her neck and winced. He seemed almost sheepish for a moment and shrugged his bony shoulders. "Sorry about that."

Adele paused for a moment, studying him. "That anger... it doesn't go away, you know..."

"That's not true," he returned.

Adele blinked.

"You never did get the bastard who did your mother, did you?"

Adele went still, motionless, just watching.

"Nah, you didn't. Otherwise you'd know. It feels like bliss. When you see the cause of everything breathing and gasping on the ground. And then breathing no more. Dead the way they did your dad—or I guess, your mother. It does make you feel better. Anyone who says otherwise is a damn liar."

"It does?" Adele said, hoarsely, swallowing back the dryness in her throat.

"One hundred percent..." His eyes gleamed wickedly for a moment, his lips curved into a small smile. But then he leaned back and shrugged. "Just... well... it doesn't last as long as you'd like. You just kinda... have to keep going, you know?"

"I was worried you'd say that."

"The one who killed your mother. You know who did it? Is he behind bars?"

"Not yet," Adele said, still quiet. "Maybe never."

"Never?" the valet asked, watching her curiously. "Never because

152

you can't find him? Or never because when you do, he won't make it to lock-up?"

Adele sat there, allowing the question to linger in the still space of the cramped car for a moment. Then she reached out, patted the valet on the leg. "I'm sorry for your loss." And before he could say anything, she pushed open the door, slipped out into the parking lot, and slammed it shut behind her.

She felt a chill shiver shudder down her spine, even though the sun was out and the air was warm. The conversation from her two partners and the German police officer seemed to have finally wound down. Judging by the look of resignation on the German officer's face, it seemed he'd finally conceded to be the one to shuttle the killer back to their precinct and finalize any paperwork.

Leoni turned, glancing around the parking lot for a moment, and then he spotted Adele once more and beamed.

"Well," he said, approaching her—though still limping—and taking both her hands. His fingers were smooth against hers and he eased his weight off his injured foot. His hands were warm and tender to the touch; she met Leoni's smiling gaze. For a moment, the sheer kindness emanating from his eyes seemed to swallow her. A kindness so unfamiliar, she almost missed it. There were no demands in those eyes—no requirements. Simply an odd affection. She felt butterflies flutter in her stomach and could feel her cheeks heating up.

"Two for two," he said with a nod. "We make a good duo, yes?"

Adele hoped desperately she wasn't blushing all of a sudden. She smiled quickly, nodding once and coughing delicately. Then she began to turn, leaving the chill emanating from the SUV behind her as she moved, leading the two men away from the German cruiser. "We do make a good team," she said.

Leoni released one of her hands but held the other, as if they were simply strolling through a park. "Ah," he said, in a tired voice. "It will be nice to sleep in my own bed again."

Adele tried not to think too much about anyone sleeping in Leoni's bed. "I understand that," she said. "You're heading back to Italy?"

"Right away, I'm afraid. The job never sleeps."

She smiled genuinely now, pushing aside her other emotions. "Neither does the agent, it seems."

Leoni let out a delicious crow of laughter, which creased his features in laugh lines. John stalked along behind both of them and his expression wasn't quite a glower, but seemed close. Adele felt uncomfortable all at once, and released Leoni's hand. She said, "Well— I certainly hope to see you again soon."

"A shared sentiment. Well, here's my ride. Do you need a lift to the airport?"

"We've got our own," John said before Adele could answer.

Leoni shrugged, indicating the black limousine that had pulled up outside the train station. A man in a white uniform stood by the doors, glancing around and pulling out a cigarette. When he noted Leoni walking over, the driver sighed, stowed his cigarette, and moved around the vehicle to open the passenger door.

Leoni waved one last time before entering the car.

Adele watched as he did, and John looked away nearly instantly, glaring at his phone and muttering to himself about *damned reception.*

"Everything okay?" Adele asked in as innocent a voice as she could muster.

"Fine," he retorted. "Taxi is on its way."

"To the airport?"

"Unless you want to take a train…"

Adele shook her head adamantly. "I think I'm done with trains."

"That we can agree on," John said.

They stood next to each other on the curb, facing the street outside the train station. For a moment, the silence stretched between them and Adele was reminded of how obnoxious she'd found Agent Renee when they'd first met. He had a prickly nature. If John decided someone was cut out of his life, he did everything in his power to keep them out.

And yet, as she stood next to the tall Frenchman, other images and memories flashed through her mind. Thoughts of when she'd first heard about Robert's illness… The way he'd comforted her, the shared moment of solace. The time when she'd been in her father's house, attacked by a killer. He'd come then too, rescuing both of them. He'd been there when they'd chased the exsanguinator, and had been there when she'd wept at the new evidence in her mother's case.

The only reason he'd been the one to glimpse her mother's killer had been because he'd wanted to solve the case… for her.

She shivered and took a half step closer to him. More a subconscious gesture than anything. She watched as Leoni's limousine pulled onto the highway, disappearing from sight.

"You all right?" John said, at last, a tinge of gentleness to his otherwise rigid tone.

"I think so," she replied, softly. "And you?"

"Fine. Taxi should be here in five."

Adele nodded softly. The sense of foreboding she'd felt had come to nothing. Maybe she really was losing her edge. The thoughts of John, the memories, came as a comfort. But also a reminder. The time she'd cried in his arms in that hotel room, learning about Robert's illness.

Robert… she needed to speak with him, and soon. She'd forgotten to touch base before leaving. He hadn't been at headquarters. She made a mental note to visit him first thing back.

CHAPTER THIRTY TWO

The painter shivered in giddy delight, his eyes once again fixed on the mansion settled behind the black gate and hedges, winking with the white marble of statuary arranged around the lawn. The lights were off now inside the mansion, though glowing orange coals could be seen, distorted through the lowest window peering into the study.

Tonight was a night of friendship. Tonight was a night of artistry.

And the savant of the Seine had eyes on his next masterpiece.

He adjusted the metallic mask he'd affixed to his face—a spit shield more than a disguise. Disguises were only needed for those who might tell tales. And the occupants of the French mansion wouldn't be speaking to anyone but the painter himself following tonight.

The painter hefted his black bag, striding forward now, feeling the odd way in which the fabric of his two sweaters rubbed against each other *and* against his hairless arms. His eyebrows were gone, his legs waxed. No DNA evidence left behind.

The painter didn't believe in half measures. A man of finality knew the risks, weighed the cost, and then set the bid.

And for him, the bid was well worth it.

He didn't hum, he didn't whistle, he didn't speak at all as he moved to the old black gate. His small, fragile form might—on the offset—look ill-suited toward acrobatic ventures. But while the painter was wire-thin, he was also fit, in a reedy sort of way, like an insect or the rigid bones found in an unearthed tomb.

He climbed the gate in three quick motions: one—a foot to the ivy-strewn wall. Two: a hand latched on the cool black metal. And finally, a pull, bringing his light form up and over, tumbling to the other side where he landed, bracing against his small, black bag.

For a moment, his single good eye fixed on a marble statue. An angel with a missing wing and a half halo stared sightlessly back at him.

The painter paused, rising slowly to his feet, staring at the statue. Then, with a snort, he reached out, shoving the angel down, burying its sculpted face into the mud, before stalking around the side of the

156

mansion, moving toward the windows of the study. Already, his gloved fingers dipped into the satchel on his hip, moving about for the tools of the trade.

***

Robert jerked awake, frowning in the night. He blinked, shaking his head, and then glanced over to the old, whittled cuckoo clock above his bed. Moonlight streamed through the window of his second-floor room, illuminating the clock and the ticking hands. The bird itself had long lain dormant, the feature disabled. But Robert liked the way the clock looked and so he kept it across from the bed. Digital sorts had never much appealed to the Frenchman.

His phone lay next to his bed, where he kept it in case of emergencies. Given recent health issues, he'd kept emergency services on speed dial. Now, though, as he lay against his pillow, staring at the moon-streaked cuckoo clock, he felt a cough forming in his throat. One a.m. Exactly.

A strange time to wake. Robert Henry had always been a bit of a night owl, but he'd also been a fastidious sleeper.

During this illness, things had changed. Basic things, like his ability to ascend the stairs to the second floor without pausing to regain his breath. Even some of the foods he'd used to enjoy would no longer stay down. He'd been minimized recently to little more than a meal of white rice and chicken broth.

Not much longer, though. Not according to the doctors.

Still, Robert wasn't the sort to give up without a fight. He wasn't particularly large, nor what others might perceive as a fighter. But he knew the game—knew how to tussle. He'd built a career off of it.

Such a silly thing, though, it seemed now. A career. So much of his life spent on a job...

But no, he reminded himself as he leaned back, holding off a cough. Not just a job. A purpose. Killers had been put to justice. And other agents he'd adopted as his own. Adele... He smiled at the memory of his pupil. She was the best of them all. He'd have to remember to give her the envelope tomorrow.

He felt a jolt of sadness she hadn't come to visit him recently, but undoubtedly the job had taken her away as it often did. Still, according to the text she'd sent the previous night, she was returning to Paris and wanted to stop by on the morrow.

Robert closed his eyes, nodding to himself, having held back the cough sufficiently. As he lay still, hoping sleep would claim him quick again, he heard the faintest of noises.

Robert's eyes snapped open. He sat up sharply, glancing toward the door. Sleep faded from him like sand drifting through a sieve, trickling out slow at first, but then in rapid proportion.

Robert's eyes fixed on the door to his room, his hand inched toward the cell phone by his bed.

No more sounds, though.

Nothing.

He shook his head, muttering to himself darkly, then leaning hesitantly back and closing his eyes again. Just the wind, then.

As Robert lay back, though, he frowned, then sat up again with a sigh. *Trust your instincts.* That's what he'd often told Adele. And his instincts were heightened now. He flung his legs over the bed, sliding his feet into his fuzzy slippers. He pulled his robe around him and then, snatching his phone, but not ringing anyone just yet, he moved slowly from his room, heading out to investigate the source of the disturbance.

***

Oh dear. Who the hell kept that many books stacked so precariously by the window ledge? The painter glared at the books blocking him from easy entry. Then, with a frown, he reached out, his fingers touching the leather spines...

He pushed, and the books tumbled to the floor. He smiled softly— sometimes art was messy. And sometimes his friends deserved a warning or two... It made it more fun that way.

The pile of fallen tomes scattered over the wooden floorboards beneath one of the red leather seats facing the dim fireplace. One of his legs was thrown through the window, the other still dangling outside, half pressed against the brick wall. He paused, listening for movement in the house.

Nothing. He couldn't hear anyone.

The painter felt a slow, growing warmth in his belly. Was he rushing this, though? Art should never be treated that way. Ought he come back? Maybe tomorrow night? No sense in rushing a masterpiece, was there? Not something this valuable. Something this

158

connected to his best of friends—Adele herself. They were bound together, he'd known this for a while. And this venture into her mentor's home was a reminder of what was at stake. The only relationship that truly mattered to him.

Still, why rush perfection?

He remained with one leg inside the mansion, the other out, caught at a crossroads, considering his options. No one had seen him—he'd avoided the two cameras in the courtyard. The only witness—the mud-streaked angel statue—was blind and dumb. Most of his friends were—at least now.

He waited a moment longer, his leg still dangling inside Robert Henry's mansion. The painter wasn't a tall man, and his foot barely brushed the floorboards beneath it.

...Could he wait longer?

No... No, art couldn't be postponed like this. Not again. He'd already waited.

No more waiting. Now was the time for work.

And with a bob of his shaved head beneath his mask, he slid fully into the study with the two red leather chairs, bringing his other leg in as well and sliding off the windowsill. He daintily stepped around the collapsed pile of books, avoiding them and slowly shutting the window until it was only cracked. He still might need the getaway—no sense providing himself an obstacle.

But still, as he glanced around the study, his single good eye flicking toward the glimmering coals in the hearth, one hand delicately braced, his glove in contact against the headrest of one of the red chairs, he allowed himself a soft smile behind his metallic mask.

It felt like a homecoming.

He looked around the silent, darkened room. Now, though, it was time to find the guest of honor. He hefted his black bag, which held the tools he'd used to enter through the window, sifting with his gloved fingers in search of other, far sharper utilities.

***

Robert's face creased in a frown. No more sounds that he could hear. No further movement. Was he just being paranoid? Were his instincts off? He'd often taught younger agents to trust their gut instincts *only if* their gut instincts had proven true in the past. Adele was a prime example. Once upon a time, he had been also. But Robert wasn't so sure anymore.

Sickness had taken much of what he'd once been. His lungs weren't as they'd used to be. Still, if someone was in the house, it would be easy enough to find them, surely. An intruder? A burglar? For a moment, he considered grabbing a knife from his office—more a letter-opener, really. But what if it was Sergeant Sharp having returned for some reason? Or maybe Adele had gotten back early and wanted to visit him.

He smiled at the thought, still holding his phone pressed against the leg of his bathrobe. He nodded to himself. Maybe it was just the wind after all. Still, it wouldn't hurt to check.

Robert took the stairs now, feeling the wood creak beneath his frail steps as he rounded the banister and moved down toward the first floor.

The sound had been muffled... the kitchen, perhaps? Maybe the study. Yes, he'd check the study first.

***

The painter could hear the creak of footsteps against the stairs. He let out a silent curse, frozen, his back pressed in the shadowy alcove behind a bookcase nearest the mantelpiece. He lodged himself in the dark, his small, frail form gifting him the ability to fit in tight spaces. His friends never expected the sorts of places he could hide. Once, even, in a suitcase beneath an older woman's bed.

He smiled. They'd never discovered that particular masterpiece. Attributed it to an animal attack. Then again, he'd gotten much better at his work since then. Every artist developed over time, given enough practice, enough focus.

And he'd practiced. Far more times than any of his friends or fans even knew.

He waited, his eyes wide, his one good eye peering out into the dark, drinking in the black and bleak of the room in every crag and cranny.

The sound of footsteps against wood had faded now. The stairs? He heard a shuffling motion, followed by a quiet, *"Merde!"*

For a moment, the painter stiffened, wondering if he'd been spotted. But then he watched as a form moved into the study, shambling along

160

in a fluffy bathrobe and slippers. A glowing device—a phone—rested against the man's leg.

Robert Henry, in the flesh. A canvas in the offering if ever he'd seen one.

The painter waited, watching, motionless as a gargoyle perched on a stone steeple.

Still muttering to himself, Robert Henry approached the fireplace and grabbed a poker. He began prodding at the glowing coals, still orange in the hearth.

"Damn it," the Frenchman muttered to himself. "Are you trying to burn the whole place down, you old fool?"

Robert jabbed and poked at the coals, extinguishing them as best he could as a scattering of dark ash settled across the brick ground beneath the hearth.

The painter shivered as he watched, staring at the movement of the man, the way his shoulders bunched, the way he lunged. More lively, more vibrant than any statue. More beautiful, more graceful than any painting.

Yes, this was why he chose this particular canvas. Flesh itself was the truest beauty to find. And true art required not just creativity, but cruelty. The courage to state the truth. To paint what one *saw*, not just what one *thought* they saw.

Satisfied he hadn't been noticed, the man stepped from the shadows, moving across the floor, stepping ever so lightly as he approached Robert from behind. Masterpieces took time. He would take his time as he always did.

And so he reached into his black bag, pulling out a thin knife. A gift the knife had been. From his first ever friend. A kingly gift, made of whale bone and pearlescent inlay. The blade itself was only six inches, yet sharp and ridged. One side for smooth strokes, the other for texture. Both involved in the creative process.

He held the knife out and stepped quietly forward, approaching Robert Henry from behind in the darkness of the mansion's gloomy study.

***

Robert heard another noise. This one from directly behind him. He went stiff, his eyes flicking away from the smoldering coals in the fire

161

toward the red leather chair nearest the window. A pile of books, some of his favorite Greek epics, had been toppled like dominoes and lay discarded across the ground.

Robert felt a prickle along his shoulder blades, his one hand gripping his phone against his thigh. He felt a shiver near his neck, this time coming from a draft ushered through the window. His eyes flitted up, still facing the fireplace, breathing shallowly as he stared toward the glass.

He'd locked that window. He knew he had.

"Please," said a voice from behind him. "Put the phone down."

Robert stiffened, his whole body going cold. *Trust your instincts.* He should have known—he should have listened. He stood for a moment in the dark, still facing the fireplace, not bearing to look at the source of the voice.

"Phone down, please," said the voice again. It wasn't snide, nor did it mock. A simple request. Not the voice of a man in search of fear. Not the voice of a cur hoping to enjoy terror. What then?

Slowly, phone still clutched in his hand, fingers trembling against the cool surface, he turned to face the source of the voice.

A small man stood across from him. Or was it a man? The voice itself was soft, lilting. Feminine? The form of the person in front of him seemed that of a child. Bone-thin, shorter, even, than Robert. Next to a man like John Renee, this fellow wouldn't have seemed any more than a child.

The figure wore a metallic mask, hiding his features, with the thinnest of holes poked in the mouth and across the lips, forming a crooked smile. Eyes glittered behind the mask, staring out the holes in the face.

"Robert," said the intruder. "Please lower your phone."

Then Robert spotted the knife. It caught in the light from the moon streaming through the open window. Robert licked the edges of his lips, feeling the roughness beneath his tongue. He kept the phone gripped, raising it a bit as if offering it to the intruder.

The masked fellow glanced down, staring at the phone. Robert's other hand, though, which had been using the poker to probe at the fireplace, gripped the iron tool behind his back, pressed against his bathrobe.

"Here," Robert said, softly. "Take it."

He didn't have time to call. Not now. Not yet. He needed the intruder distracted, though.

The masked fellow tipped his head sideways, as if confused by a spectacle. He reached out with his free hand, gloved, groping toward Robert's offered phone. The old DGSI agent waited a moment, waiting for contact, waiting for those twig-like fingers to wrap around his phone.

Then, as the intruder pulled the device away, his knife dipping just a bit, Robert swung with all his might. The poker whipped around, streaking toward where the masked man stood. Robert shouted with the exertion.

But he missed.

The masked man was fast—far faster than Robert had anticipated. One moment he'd been standing still, it seemed, holding Robert's phone, cradling it in one hand. The next, he darted *forward*. Rather than lunging back to avoid the blow, he lurched *closer*. The poker hit the man's thin shoulder, but the momentum near the base was nearly nothing and it ricocheted harmlessly.

Robert cried out in pain, his fingers aching all of a sudden. The frail form of the intruder tutted, drawn in close. Two eyes, one of them dim and dull, flashed behind the metal mask. "Bad boy," said the intruder, giggling now. And then he jammed his knife into Robert's arm.

The poker dropped, clattering to the floor.

Robert cursed and tried to shove the killer off him. But despite the frailty of the intruder, Robert felt his own weakness come upon him all of a sudden, like a freezing glaze of ice, stopping all motion and chilling his bones.

Robert gasped now, bleeding from his stabbed arm, staring up at the metallic mask. It took him a moment to realize he was now on his knees, trying to catch his bearings, his legs having given out from the adrenaline of it all.

"You're weak, old friend," said the intruder, softly. "Pliable. A perfect canvas."

"Fuck off," Robert snapped, staring up and gasping. He began to cough, the sudden flood of rapid air in his lungs stimulating them to reject the flood of pressure.

As he coughed, gasping, he dropped to his hands, his knees still rough against the floorboards.

He looked up and glimpsed the metallic face twist, staring down at him.

"Who are you?" Robert said, though he had a guess.

"A friend," the man said, cheerfully. The knife was still clutched in one gloved hand, Robert's phone in the other.

Robert stared at the glowing device, bleeding from his arm, feeling droplets speckle the floorboards. He winced, glaring up. For a moment, he faked another cough, if only to have an excuse to bunch up, preparing to lunge in one last desperate attempt for that phone.

But the masked man seemed to sense Robert's intent and skipped back, again far too quickly, like a dancer.

Robert's fingers swiped empty air and he landed face first, chin jamming against the rough floor. He felt one of his old books pressed beneath his ribs. He could feel blood swelling down his arm now.

The killer was murmuring to himself, scrolling through Robert's phone, which was left unlocked during the night in case of a medical emergency. Now, though, it allowed the killer to scroll through his texts. The bastard paused at once, going stiff.

"Adele," he said, uttering the word breathlessly like a lover at the sight of his bride. He looked up now, his eyes—the one dull, the one vibrant—staring out from the metallic mask. "She is coming tomorrow?"

"I don't know who Adele is," Robert spat. "Wrong number."

The intruder laughed, a hearty, authentic sound. He shook his head and chuckled, holding the phone a moment and then pressing it into his pocket. "It will be nice to talk to Adele," said the killer. "In a way she'll receive it. It isn't fun to go without seeing one's friends for so long."

Robert snarled now, trying to rise, but finding his injured arm insufficient to bear his weight. "You leave her alone! Hear me? Leave her out of this, you sick twist!"

The intruder paused, contemplating these words. Then his expression behind the mask seemed to darken, as if a light dimmed in his eyes. "I don't think I will, thank you," he said, quietly. "Adele and I have unfinished business. And I'm afraid you're standing in the way. Don't worry, Mr. Henry, we only have tonight together. I wish it were a week, maybe two. But I'll have to work with the time we have."

And then the intruder stepped forward, fast—far too fast, his knife flashing down, a foot planting firmly in Robert's weakened chest and shoving him back against the floorboards in his own home.

All that remained was a glimmer of regret, sheer fear, and a white-hot anger with nowhere left to go.

Then... all of these faded too, replaced by a sudden cold.

CHAPTER THIRTY THREE

Adele slumped more than strolled out of the sliding glass doors of the airport, John Renee marching at her side. She glanced at her phone. Two a.m. Night had fallen complete and beckoned starlight in coaxing breaths from the ebony horizon.

Adele paused on the sidewalk outside the airport, listening to the quiet buzz of airplanes in the background. The sparse terminal itself had emptied rather quickly, leaving Adele and John both standing by the curb, witnessed only by a distant traffic warden leaning against an old security vehicle and chatting with a guard through the window.

John sighed, glancing at his phone and muttering, "Ride is going to be late," he murmured. Then, after a moment, he added, "Sorry."

Adele glanced up at Renee where he stood illuminated by the safety lights above the sign for the terminal. His scars traced the underside of his chin and his eyes fixed on the asphalt ahead of them, flicking expectantly toward the roundabout where the passenger vehicles would come to pick up their fares.

"It's all right," she murmured quietly, closing her eyes for a moment and resisting the urge to rest against John. She was so tired. The airplane ride had proceeded in the same quiet that had existed between them for the last few days.

A quiet she'd grown to hate, but one she didn't quite know how to shatter.

She looked up again, and the tall Frenchman was staring at her. She blinked, looked away, glanced back, and now John was looking off at the road again, as if embarrassed she'd caught him watching.

"What is it?" she asked, offering the question like a gift, but also wincing as if fearful he might slap it away.

John, though, just sighed and regarded her for a moment with a soft, sad glimmer to his gaze. "I was just thinking," he said, standing in the quiet.

"Thinking about what?"

"Nothing," he murmured. "Nothing important."

Adele nodded, feeling a flutter of disappointment. Again, in the distance she heard the churn of an airplane engine, listening as it carried the aircraft away and over the airport.

Adele sighed softly to herself, her mind wandering away in the cool darkness of the isolated terminal. "John," she ventured softly, her eyes flitting up to him once again,

"What?" John said, his tone similarly hesitant, it seemed. She tried to remember if he'd had more than one drink on the plane, but couldn't recollect.

She met his gaze, her own heart still. He looked back, his expression soft for the first time, it seemed, in weeks.

"John," she murmured.

"Adele?"

She swallowed, then said, "You... you can be a right bastard sometimes, you know that?"

John blinked, then frowned. He turned now, facing her, feet set at shoulder width. His eyes flashed for a moment and he sniffed. "What the hell do you mean?" he demanded.

Adele shrugged now, looking away and staring out across the abandoned terminal. She looked to her phone. It was 2:05 now. Too late to have this conversation. Too late for much. Then again, she'd never been able to muster up the courage to confront him during the day, while on the job. If not now, then when?

"You are," she insisted. "But... not in a bad way. Not really. I sometimes think I have you figured out, but then you go and do something that makes me question it."

"Ah, the trait of every bastard then."

"I'm not joking. You're impossible. But useful. You act like I don't exist anymore. And yet you still have my back when I need you. You're a strange one, John Renee." Adele wasn't sure where this sudden spurt of honesty was coming from, but she also didn't want to lose the current of it, so she pressed into the words, her brow furrowing as she did.

"I... I think I'm sorry," she said. "For how I treated you after... well..."

"After I let your mother's killer get away?"

"Yes." Adele bit her lip. "But you saved a life. That's all we can do sometimes. You saved a life. I'm sorry for treating you like... well..."

"Like a bastard."

"I guess so."

John stood with his eyes fixed on her, solemn and sincere. "I... I thought you were tired of me," he murmured, quietly. Now he turned, facing the road again, as if plotting an escape route. "It doesn't matter." He went still, quiet.

"No," she insisted, propelled by some summoned courage from a hidden place. She didn't know why she was pressing, why she wouldn't let it go. But in that same moment, she realized she didn't want to. She knew John—and when he acted like himself, his true self, there was no one she trusted more. When he acted like a shadow of himself, he was the most obnoxious, unprofessional, ridiculous man she'd ever known. It was infuriating...

And yet part of her enjoyed the two-sided coin that was Renee's personality. Part of her also loathed it. For a brief moment, she thought of Agent Leoni. Of Christopher. His kindness, his self-sacrifice, his willingness to care about her regardless of what she seemed to do.

She felt a flutter of guilt and frustration in her stomach, and she glanced off now, staring at the road heading in the opposite direction from John's own gaze. Both of them continued to stare in different directions for a moment. And John muttered, "Taxi should be here soon."

"Great."

"Yeah. Great."

Adele waited, hesitant. She hadn't known what she wanted John to say, but silence wasn't it. She'd broken open the dam, cracked the seal, voided the warranty, as it were. Now, it was John's turn. But what had she expected? It wasn't like Renee was a wind-up toy she could force into her bidding at a moment's notice. Hell, half the time, John didn't seem to have rhyme or reason behind *anything* he did. And yet he was an effective agent.

An effective companion... after a style.

The silence continued a bit longer, and Adele found herself getting angry. She didn't even understand why, and yet as John refused to speak, as she stared off and away from him, her imagination churning, her own mind began to grow restless. Her lips drew in a thin line and she muttered. "Damn it, Renee. Why can't you ever just say what's—"

"I hate what you do," he said, suddenly, interrupting her.

Adele blinked and turned back now. Both of them were watching each other like two cats in the dark, searching out the boundaries of new territory.

168

"How nice of you to say," Adele murmured.

"You're the one who called me a bastard."

"I did that for emphasis."

"So am I. I do hate what you do. I hate…" He hesitated, scratching at his jaw, but this time not quite looking away. "I hate how you make me feel."

Adele blinked, staring now. She found her breath came a little more quickly.

John gritted his teeth, his jaw stretched, the scars along his chin standing out rigid and pale in the poorly illuminated outside terminal. He sighed, then passed a hand through his hair. "Christ, Adele," he said. "You're a strange one—I'll give you that. I wish I didn't… you know… care." He shook his head as if puzzled. "Really, I do," he added, glancing back at her as if in emphasis. "But you're just… you're an odd bird, aren't you? You're… You're…" He sighed and shrugged.

"An odd bird," Adele said, softly, trying not to smile. "What every girl wants to hear."

"I might not be able to tell you what I'm thinking… but I know how you make me feel," he said, nodding adamantly. "That Leoni fellow, he's an asshole. I hated him. Hated him the moment I saw him. Couldn't quite place why, to be honest with you. Then I saw him hold your hand, and I swear, Adele…" John inhaled deeply. "I swear I wanted to put a bullet in him then and there."

"John!"

"I didn't—just to be clear. Need I remind you? I didn't. But also, the thought of him driving us to the airport. Of taking us in that stupid limousine." John shuddered, shaking his head. "I could've punched him."

Adele hesitated, feeling a panic rising in her. Was this what she wanted to hear? Part of her thought so, another part wished he would shut up, or lie. But in that moment, ever the investigator, her curiosity got the better of her. She said, softly, "John… I don't care what you think about Leoni. I know what you're trying to say. But I want you to say it. Leave Leoni out of it. Leave your anger at the door, just for one moment. Can you do that? Or is it so much a part of you, you're not even able—"

"God damn it. Just shut up, will you," John growled. Then he leaned in, reminding her once again just how tall the Frenchman was. He didn't hesitate, he didn't ask, he didn't do anything or speak any more words except place his arm around her lower back and press his lips to hers.

The faintest of moments passed where she could have pulled away, where she felt his breath against her cheeks, warm and soft.

And then, he pulled her in complete. For a moment, the two of them stood there, beneath the flickering lights of the airport terminal. John holding her close, sharing breath, their mouths drinking the other in. The warmth from him, the scent of smooth cologne and sweat. The sound of his breathing, the gentle gust of air from his nose against her cheek as he exhaled a soft sound of pleasure.

He leaned in, holding her tighter now, practically lifting her from her feet. The kiss itself seemed so... John. Aggressive, passionate, intense. There was a sort of kindled rage to it as well, a declaration—it seemed—a howl against any who might intrude on that moment, intrude on the space between them. But there was no space, not where John was concerned. His frame blocked out any glimpses of shimmering fluorescent lights, his back to the road now, fully facing her at last.

They remained like that, the intensity rising and falling in swells like rolling waves dashed against the shore. For a moment, Adele felt a flicker along her back where his fingers pressed, felt a sense of tingling along her spine.

John Renee... unprofessional, obnoxious. But damn, was he a good kisser.

Not the first time, but this second kiss was more... *honest*... than the first.

At last, though, she pulled back, panting and staring up at him wide-eyed. He didn't blink, didn't look away, but also breathed, gasping, his chest heaving as if he'd just sprinted up a flight of stairs. A faint flicker of delight flashed across his eyes, the corners of his lips turned up into a sort of tomcat grin. He winked at her. "Call me a bastard again," he murmured.

Adele stared back.

"Come on, Adele," John probed. "Call me—"

This time, it was her turn to roll her eyes and mutter, "Shut up." She leaned in, hard, giving just as much of the fire, the fury, as he'd provided, leaning into him. She shared her breath with his, feeling the way his lips fit to hers, soft and yet rigid. The way he leaned in, hard, his eyes closed the moment they drew too near. Her own eyes flickered,

170

flashing and casting images of his features like through an old projection screen across her vision.

At last, when she was good and ready, she let him go, stepping back and staring at him. This time, she flashed a grin and also winked for good measure.

Even in this shared embrace, it seemed impossible to fully put aside the edge to their relationship. And perhaps that's what made it intoxicating.

"Well then," John murmured.

"Well then," Adele returned.

She paused, breathing, gathering her thoughts. She watched John, staring at him, frozen in that delightful moment a second longer. She didn't want to leave it. It seemed a warm cocoon, a shield from the rest of the world, from... everything.

But like all cocoons, this one began to shatter the moment she heard the squeak of taxi wheels against the road. She glanced over and spotted two cabs coming down the road outside the terminal. She blinked, and glanced at John.

"Called two," he murmured in matter of explanation. "Figured we'd be going opposite directions."

Adele nodded, biting her lower lip and frowning for a moment. She thought of Leoni, of his offer for a ride to the airport. Of the way he listened, the way he seemed to care about what she thought. He had limped along the train, following after them with gritted teeth. A liability more than anything on that case.

But did that matter at all?

John was an agent, through and through. A reliable partner, dangerous in battle and trustworthy in a fox hole.

But was that what she wanted? The cocoon seemed shattered completely now. John almost seemed to sense it, and his eyes narrowed, flicking from the nearest taxi to her. He exhaled softly. Then, as if in manner of explanation, he murmured. "I wish I didn't feel this way," he said. "I wish I didn't, but I do. And I thought you should know." He reached up, teeth pressed against his lower lip as if in thought. Then he shrugged, turned, and approached the nearest taxi. "Good night, American Princess," he called over his shoulder. "I'll see you around."

The warmth was gone, the cocoon had vanished, and once more she stood on the cold, hard sidewalk, numb and frowning, watching John

Renee enter the taxi and watching him instruct the driver. A moment later, the vehicle pulled away, leaving her standing in front of the second cab that pulled to the curb.

She leaned down, picking up her carry-on and laptop bag and sighing into the night. She could still just about smell his cologne. What did any of that even mean? He wished he *didn't* feel that way?

Did she?

Adele didn't know what she wished. Which was half the trouble.

Adele sighed, shaking her head and stepping toward the taxi, entering the back passenger seat. She wasn't in the mood for conversation.

"Where to?" the cabbie asked, glancing in the rearview mirror.

Adele paused, began to answer, but then frowned as her phone vibrated.

She glanced down. Nearly two thirty in the morning now. They'd been standing outside the airport for nearly half an hour.

Damn.

She shook her head in exhaustion, but then stared at the notification on her phone. A message. Her frown settled, and she felt a sudden flutter of the same sense of foreboding that had been haunting her ever since she'd left the DGSI headquarters two days ago.

But as she opened the message, she sighed in relief.

From Robert Henry. The words were short, to the point, sent only a minute ago.

Land yet? Could you come visit? I have something I need to show you.

Adele stared at the message. She paused, shaking her head, and muttered to the cabbie. "Sorry, one second."

Then she texted back. *Right now?*

A pause as she stared at the blank phone.

Then three words flashed across the text chain.

Right now, please.

Adele stared at the glowing white light from her phone inside the still taxi. She felt a flicker of tiredness try to compete with her other emotions. *Couldn't it wait, Robert?* She thought to herself. So late at night? Then again, she'd always known Agent Henry to be a night owl. She smiled, recollecting moments by the fireplace, reading books together well into the morning, sitting in those twin red leather chairs. She remembered more than one bowl of chocolate cereal late at night, discussing politics or philosophy or simply listening to Robert share old war stories from his younger years.

Two thirty in the morning wasn't *so* late. Not for Robert. Besides, she'd wanted to see him when she got back any way.

"All right, sorry," Adele said, quickly, glancing up into the mirror again. She pushed her phone into her pocket and then provided the taxi driver with Robert Henry's address. "It's a big place," she added. "Lot of statues in the garden."

The driver nodded once, plotting the course on his GPS, and Adele leaned back in the passenger seat, staring out the window and smiling at the thought of reuniting with her old mentor.

CHAPTER THIRTY FOUR

The taxi rolled to a gentle stop on the curb outside Robert's mansion.

"This it?" the driver asked, glancing in the rearview mirror and waiting expectantly.

"Yeah, thanks," Adele said, handing a fifty-euro note to the man and adding, "Keep the change."

The driver gave a quick nod of gratitude as Adele extricated herself, her carry-on, and her laptop bag from the back seat. She turned away as the taxi wheeled softly out the of the suburb on the outskirts of Paris. Adele paused for a moment, staring up at Robert's old home, her eyes flicking along the statues in the yard. She felt a flush of relief, like slipping into a warm bath. It was a homecoming of sorts, and for a moment, she closed her eyes, thinking to all the moments and times she'd missed this place and her old mentor, also recollecting the times she'd spent here, just her and Robert, alone in the mansion, reading books, laughing, *living.*

She sighed softly at this final thought. Remembering the way Robert had looked in that hospital bed, draped in the gown of death. He'd been so shriveled, so small, so weak. She hated the thought of her old mentor in pain. Hated contemplating what he was going through.

She pressed the buzzer at the gate and waited quietly.

A moment passed, then another. She frowned, her eyes flicking toward the old mansion. The light was on inside the study, beaming through a cracked window.

"Robert?" she called, her voice faint in the darkness.

No answer.

She glanced at her phone—no new texts. She buzzed the intercom again.

Nothing.

Three a.m. now. Nearly a half hour since he'd invited her over. Had Robert fallen asleep? For a moment she considered leaving, letting her old mentor get his rest. But then her eyes flitted to the light inside the mansion, and she went still.

Robert wasn't the sort to leave a light on. He was very conscious about that sort of thing. And why was the window open? Again, not something Robert would do before falling asleep—he was a security snob too. Hence the cameras, the gate, and the alarm system on the front and back doors.

"Robert?" she called, a bit louder this time, then glancing sheepishly toward a couple of the other enormous houses across the street.

No lights from within those. Only a single beacon of illumination streaming through Robert's window.

Adele sighed, raised her phone, and called her old mentor.

She waited as the dial tone continued ringing in the background. Her eyes flitted through the black marble bars, settling on one of the statues. A small marble angel had been toppled, planted face-first in the mud.

"Robert?" Adele called a bit louder now, facing the open window and still hearing the sound of the ring tone in her ear.

After another few rings, she hung up and stared at the fence.

"Great," she muttered to herself. She leaned her laptop bag and old carry-on against the ivy-covered wall and backed up a few steps, preparing for a running start. Vaguely, she was reminded of a case when she'd broken into an alley behind an auto shop with John. They'd climbed a fence then too.

She smiled for a moment, still angled toward the gate.

John Renee was a strange one. An odd combination of infuriating and intoxicating...

She paused now, one foot off the curb, prepared for a running start. For a moment, she considered John. Considered her father. Considered it all.

Her mother's killer had driven a rift between her and Renee. Had highlighted the cracks in the relationship she shared with her father. She'd made it all so personal. Focused far too much on the killer as a monster, as someone worthy of retribution. And yet he was a person. Just like the other murderers, just like the valet.

She shook her head, one foot still off the curb, braced on the street where she faced the gate. Her eyes slipped toward the crumpled strap of her abandoned laptop bag and the carry-on. No one in this neighborhood would take them. No one would likely even be awake.

She lowered her head for a moment, feeling her lips tingle as memories surfaced, playing across her mind's eye and bringing with them a thought of John. She'd kissed him back. But did she regret it?

She didn't know what she thought. John was a man in motion—a form of action in and of himself. And yet was that the life she wanted? Forever? Did she want to live in a way that required the level of danger John seemed to crave?

Did she even want to continue this job forever? Adele sighed. She didn't like where her mind wandered so late at night.

Regardless, she'd made it too personal. Too personal with John, too personal with her father—not the relationships themselves, but the *impact* they had on the case. The impact, more importantly, the case had on the relationships. Her mother was dead. Ten years had passed. The killer was out there, likely retreating, hiding in the shadows, disappearing from the radar of any law enforcement agency.

A ghost in the wind.

She'd been left with dust at her fingertips. She couldn't allow it to remain so personal. It would consume her alive.

With a reluctant, but strengthening nod, Adele focused on the gate once more. Glanced through the cracked window into the study, where light was still shining, and then, when Robert didn't buzz the gate, she broke into a sprint, taking the three wild strides to cover the distance between the curb and the steel bars.

She flung herself at the gate and in three quick motions, kicked off the stone wall covered in ivy, snared the top of the metal barrier, and pulled herself up and over, vaulting the barricade and landing with a dull *thump* on the other side, facing Robert's garden.

Adele brushed the dust off her hands and smiled to herself, moving rapidly toward the front of the mansion. She passed the fallen angel in the mud and paused for a moment, reaching down and plucking up the marble creation, setting it back up as it had been. She frowned at the mud and dirt streaking the sculpted features and, dropping low, she rubbed her sleeve in the grooves of the statue's face, removing the grime and mud as best she could. Some of it fell away, but mostly it just streaked the statue.

She sighed and shrugged to herself. It was the best she could do; she'd just have to mention it to Robert so he could clean the statue properly.

She moved across the flagstones, through the garden and toward a row of hedges beneath the open window facing the study. She couldn't spot the fire in the fireplace, but did note the overhead chandelier buzzing with electricity and illuminating the room beyond. Adele frowned, leaning toward the open window.

"Robert!" she called.

No answer.

"Robert!" She raised her voice, now feeling a prickle of fear claw its way up her spine. She checked her phone again. No texts, no calls.

The fear came like a flash flood, bringing with it all manner of horrible imaginings regarding her old mentor and friend. Had his sickness finally overtaken him? What if he was in the bath somewhere, gasping for breath, desperate for help?

Adele cursed and bounded up the steps to the front door. She reached out, slamming a hand against the brass knocker and jamming a finger into the buzzer. The two sounds broke rhythmically in the night. One moment, a faint humming buzz from within, the next a deep, bellowing knock from the door itself.

Again, no response, no answer—the door remained sealed.

"Damn it, Robert!" Adele said, her fear rising in her gut.

For a moment, she considered calling the emergency services. But then inwardly kicked herself. "That's *you*, dummy," she muttered to herself.

She tried the knocker one last time, but when it did nothing, she reached down and pulled on the door handle. Locked.

"Damn it," she repeated, this time breaking into a jog, taking the stairs two at a time and rapidly approaching the hedge beneath the open window. Robert would understand, certainly. She'd once crept into the house, nearly five years ago, by climbing through a second-story window. He'd understood then—even laughed about it with her—and he'd understand now. Robert always did.

She flung herself over the windowsill, but then went still. One leg dangled inside the room, the other still wedged against the brick wall, pushed against the prickling branches and jutting branches of the bush itself.

"Hello," she murmured, her eyes fixed on the window.

Someone had drawn a heart on the window. Was that lipstick? She leaned in, staring at the small heart, seemingly sketched haphazardly against the glass.

No. Not lipstick.

Her stomach flipped and she went so cold she thought she might

177

fall from her perch. Her eyes fixed unblinking on the small sketch of the red heart in the bottom frame of the open window.

Blood. Someone had drawn a heart in blood.

Her own heart pounded fiercely in her chest, and she lifted her eyes slowly, turning toward the illuminated study.

"Robert..." she murmured, softly, feeling a prickle along her arms and up her spine.

Her eyes fell on the red leather chair furthest from the window. The same chair she normally used when at Robert's home. She stared at it, blinking.

"Robert," she murmured, softly...

Her old mentor was sitting in the chair, eyes open, staring up at the ceiling. Adele swallowed. "Robert?" she said a bit more loudly. Slowly, trembling, she brought her second leg through the window, nearly slipping on a pile of toppled books. Greek classics, by the looks of them—Robert's favorite.

She stared at where her old mentor reclined in the leather chair.

Except it was the wrong chair. He wouldn't have chosen the one nearest the kitchen. A man of habit, was her old mentor.

She murmured his name again, eyes fixed on his form, stepping forward. No movement. No breath. His chest wasn't rising or falling. She felt a flicker of sheer horror rising in her. Absolute despair flooded her stomach.

"Ro—Ro—" This time, the word didn't manage to leave her lips. It died somewhere in her throat as she drew near and went still.

His chair was encircled with a small puddle of water... Well, not small, she realized as she drew within touch. Not a puddle of water either...

More blood, circling Robert's chair like a crimson halo against the floorboards.

Blood from where?

She reached out with trembling fingers, feeling the horror of the moment slowly wash across her back, tingling along her spine and coming to her scalp in vibrant pulses. She gasped in shattered breaths, her fingers groping the fabric of his bathrobe. "I... I..." she murmured unable to say anything in its fullness.

She slowly opened Robert's robe and realized now his mouth was twisted, frozen in an agonized scream, his eyes facing up at the ceiling, dead, lifeless.

The flap of his rope opened, falling aside and revealing her old mentor's bare chest gouged with cuts and laced with swirling patterns of ruined flesh. Adele screamed then, shouting in equal parts shock and blistering agony.

She stumbled back, slipping on her old mentor's blood and falling on her hands. She scrambled back as if to distance herself from the spectacle alone, but her eyes refused to budge. They remained glued to Robert's tortured, disfigured form. She spotted one of his hands now, resting on the table next to him. Missing three of its fingers. She spotted where his lips, his cheeks, everything about her old mentor, had been torn about, ripped to shreds, cut and carved in swirling patterns of bloody flesh.

"Dear Christ," she muttered. "Christ, Christ—damn it!" she screamed.

Adele leaned back, gasping, her chest heaving, her back against the brick fireplace as she stared at the ruined corpse of her old mentor. The small heart etched in Robert's blood was visible just out of the corner of her eye. Gasping, growling now, feeling a feral ferocity rise in her chest, Adele staggered to her feet, leaving bloody footprints beneath her where she'd stepped.

"No..." she murmured, breathing heavily. "No. No. No." But the words themselves seemed futile. She stepped forward now, staggering toward the corpse of her old mentor. The anger was fleeting though. It had promised support, strength, but then fled as she drew near, leaving her only with an emptiness in her gut.

She gasped, choking out a sob, and found hot tears suddenly flooding down her cheeks.

A crime scene... Don't touch him, dummy. The voice in her head wasn't loud enough, though. The shock alone seemed to be pulsing with prickles through her skull.

"Christ," she muttered. "No. No..." No other words seemed to come, nothing concrete fell from her lips. She stumbled toward Robert, reaching out and gripping at his chest with one hand, her fingers coming away soaked in the blood that stained his bathrobe. She collapsed at his knees.

"No, no, no," she cried, her voice strangled. She sobbed now, shaking, her chin resting against her old mentor's knees. Feeling, beneath her own chin, where even his legs hadn't been spared the torture.

179

She collapsed, leaning against Robert's corpse, gasping and heaving sobs into his lap, gasping and gasping, unable to breathe, unable to speak.

She'd been wrong.

The killer hadn't fled. He hadn't gone into hiding. She didn't want to make it personal.

So he had.

He had come, he had taken, and he had left a small little heart etched in her true father's window. A coy little invitation, a playful gesture, asking for her to look closer, to peel back the curtains and peer through the window.

But some sights were best left unseen.

No. He hadn't gone into hiding at all. He was fully back now. He'd done this... *because of her.*

She gasped, sobbing, weeping, unable to rise, unable to extricate herself from the frayed form of Robert Henry, her tears dappling his blood-soaked garments, her breath gasping against his broken form.

The choice was gone. She couldn't step back now. It was personal. Deeply personal.

One way or another, this wouldn't end in a courtroom. It had started in blood, and it would end the same. Adele clenched her teeth, snarling now and gasping, desperately trembling as her fingers reached for her phone to call... call who? No one could help. Robert was gone.

Her mother was gone.

And the bastard who'd taken them was laughing.

NOW AVAILABLE!

LEFT TO VANISH
(An Adele Sharp Mystery—Book 8)

"When you think that life cannot get better, Blake Pierce comes up with another masterpiece of thriller and mystery! This book is full of twists and the end brings a surprising revelation. I strongly recommend this book to the permanent library of any reader that enjoys a very well written thriller."
--Books and Movie Reviews, Roberto Mattos (re Almost Gone)

LEFT TO VANISH is book #8 in a new FBI thriller series featuring Adele Sharp (the series begins with LEFT TO DIE, book #1) by USA Today bestselling author Blake Pierce, whose #1 bestseller Once Gone (a free download) has received over 1,000 five star reviews.

When a seemingly unconnected string of murders occurs in vacation homes scattered throughout the French countryside, many involving American, German and Italian expats, FBI Special Agent Adele Sharp—triple agent of the U.S., France and Germany—is called in to cross borders and use her brilliant mind to figure out who is behind it.

Are the murders coincidental?

Or are they the work of a single, deranged serial killer?

And can Adele stop him before he strikes again?

An action-packed mystery series of international intrigue and riveting suspense, LEFT TO VANISH will leave you turning pages late into the night.

Books #9 and #10 in the series—LEFT TO HUNT and LEFT TO FEAR—are now also available!

LEFT TO VANISH
(An Adele Sharp Mystery—Book 8)

Did you know that I've written multiple novels in the mystery genre? If you haven't read all my series, click the image below to download a series starter!

Blake Pierce

Blake Pierce is the USA Today bestselling author of the RILEY PAGE mystery series, which includes seventeen books. Blake Pierce is also the author of the MACKENZIE WHITE mystery series, comprising fourteen books; of the AVERY BLACK mystery series, comprising six books; of the KERI LOCKE mystery series, comprising five books; of the MAKING OF RILEY PAIGE mystery series, comprising six books; of the KATE WISE mystery series, comprising seven books; of the CHLOE FINE psychological suspense mystery, comprising six books; of the JESSE HUNT psychological suspense thriller series, comprising fifteen books (and counting); of the AU PAIR psychological suspense thriller series, comprising three books; of the ZOE PRIME mystery series, comprising six books; of the ADELE SHARP mystery series, comprising ten books (and counting); of the EUROPEAN VOYAGE cozy mystery series, comprising six books (and counting); of the new LAURA FROST FBI suspense thriller, comprising three books (and counting); of the new ELLA DARK FBI suspense thriller, comprising six books (and counting); of the A YEAR IN EUROPE cozy mystery series, comprising three books (and counting); of the AVA GOLD mystery series, comprising three books (and counting); and of the RACHEL GIFT mystery series, comprising three books (and counting).

An avid reader and lifelong fan of the mystery and thriller genres, Blake loves to hear from you, so please feel free to visit www.blakepierceauthor.com to learn more and stay in touch.

BOOKS BY BLAKE PIERCE

RACHEL GIFT MYSTERY SERIES
HER LAST WISH (Book #1)
HER LAST CHANCE (Book #2)
HER LAST HOPE (Book #3)

AVA GOLD MYSTERY SERIES
CITY OF PREY (Book #1)
CITY OF FEAR (Book #2)
CITY OF BONES (Book #3)

A YEAR IN EUROPE
A MURDER IN PARIS (Book #1)
DEATH IN FLORENCE (Book #2)
VENGEANCE IN VIENNA (Book #3)

ELLA DARK FBI SUSPENSE THRILLER
GIRL, ALONE (Book #1)
GIRL, TAKEN (Book #2)
GIRL, HUNTED (Book #3)
GIRL, SILENCED (Book #4)
GIRL, VANISHED (Book 5)
GIRL ERASED (Book #6)

LAURA FROST FBI SUSPENSE THRILLER
ALREADY GONE (Book #1)
ALREADY SEEN (Book #2)
ALREADY TRAPPED (Book #3)

EUROPEAN VOYAGE COZY MYSTERY SERIES
MURDER (AND BAKLAVA) (Book #1)
DEATH (AND APPLE STRUDEL) (Book #2)
CRIME (AND LAGER) (Book #3)
MISFORTUNE (AND GOUDA) (Book #4)
CALAMITY (AND A DANISH) (Book #5)
MAYHEM (AND HERRING) (Book #6)

ADELE SHARP MYSTERY SERIES
LEFT TO DIE (Book #1)

LEFT TO RUN (Book #2)
LEFT TO HIDE (Book #3)
LEFT TO KILL (Book #4)
LEFT TO MURDER (Book #5)
LEFT TO ENVY (Book #6)
LEFT TO LAPSE (Book #7)
LEFT TO VANISH (Book #8)
LEFT TO HUNT (Book #9)
LEFT TO FEAR (Book #10)

THE AU PAIR SERIES
ALMOST GONE (Book#1)
ALMOST LOST (Book #2)
ALMOST DEAD (Book #3)

ZOE PRIME MYSTERY SERIES
FACE OF DEATH (Book#1)
FACE OF MURDER (Book #2)
FACE OF FEAR (Book #3)
FACE OF MADNESS (Book #4)
FACE OF FURY (Book #5)
FACE OF DARKNESS (Book #6)

A JESSIE HUNT PSYCHOLOGICAL SUSPENSE SERIES
THE PERFECT WIFE (Book #1)
THE PERFECT BLOCK (Book #2)
THE PERFECT HOUSE (Book #3)
THE PERFECT SMILE (Book #4)
THE PERFECT LIE (Book #5)
THE PERFECT LOOK (Book #6)
THE PERFECT AFFAIR (Book #7)
THE PERFECT ALIBI (Book #8)
THE PERFECT NEIGHBOR (Book #9)
THE PERFECT DISGUISE (Book #10)
THE PERFECT SECRET (Book #11)
THE PERFECT FAÇADE (Book #12)
THE PERFECT IMPRESSION (Book #13)
THE PERFECT DECEIT (Book #14)
THE PERFECT MISTRESS (Book #15)

ONCE SHUNNED (Book #15)
ONCE MISSED (Book #16)
ONCE CHOSEN (Book #17)

MACKENZIE WHITE MYSTERY SERIES
BEFORE HE KILLS (Book #1)
BEFORE HE SEES (Book #2)
BEFORE HE COVETS (Book #3)
BEFORE HE TAKES (Book #4)
BEFORE HE NEEDS (Book #5)
BEFORE HE FEELS (Book #6)
BEFORE HE SINS (Book #7)
BEFORE HE HUNTS (Book #8)
BEFORE HE PREYS (Book #9)
BEFORE HE LONGS (Book #10)
BEFORE HE LAPSES (Book #11)
BEFORE HE ENVIES (Book #12)
BEFORE HE STALKS (Book #13)
BEFORE HE HARMS (Book #14)

AVERY BLACK MYSTERY SERIES
CAUSE TO KILL (Book #1)
CAUSE TO RUN (Book #2)
CAUSE TO HIDE (Book #3)
CAUSE TO FEAR (Book #4)
CAUSE TO SAVE (Book #5)
CAUSE TO DREAD (Book #6)

KERI LOCKE MYSTERY SERIES
A TRACE OF DEATH (Book #1)
A TRACE OF MUDER (Book #2)
A TRACE OF VICE (Book #3)
A TRACE OF CRIME (Book #4)
A TRACE OF HOPE (Book #5)